THE NUMBER CONSPIRACY

Printed in the United States of America

Printing, 2013, 2016

ISBN 978-0692815816

Ingram Content Group Inc.
1 Ingram Boulevard, La Vergne, Tennessee 37086
(615) 793-5000
IngramContent.com

Preface

This book is dedicated to the people who made the ultimate sacrifices to do what's right to make a difference. I would like to thank everyone who have supported me throughout the years including my family and my friends, special thanks to my mother for helping with the editing. I dream to become an inspiration in good terms, but things have also inspired me as well. Throughout history, there have been people that have made choices to help others, but some of those people have had to pay the ultimate price. Even heroes can be just as vulnerable as a regular citizen. Some people have died because they had a purpose in life, to

protect our rights as people, to be who we are today and

where we stand as a whole. The list goes on with the

numerous types of problems that make up our world today.

Throughout life, we have to make choices, even if it has to do

with making sacrifices for the sake of protecting someone

else. We have to keep moving forward. You have to be strong

and keep your head up, because somewhere out there, the

world is a dangerous place.

In Loving Memory of

Ralph William Giovannone (1950 - 2007)

Introduction

July 19, 2019

They arrive at the door on a Friday, sunny afternoon. A man gets an unexpected visit from two people dressed in black while disguised as government officials. The man wore a white dress shirt with black dress pants, shoes and tie. The officials wore a white dress shirt with black ties over their shirts along with their black suit jackets. The black official had short black hair. The white official has blonde hair that stuck up throughout his scalp while wearing a pair of sunglasses. "Your number's up, you need to come with us," the black official said.

"What the hell are you guys talking about? Who are you and what are you doing here? Explain yourself or I'm calling the police!"

"Sir, that's not important right now. We work for the government. We get engaged in federal and governmental activity all the time. We are the police." The man didn't buy what the black official said. The man told them one more time to get off of his property, "I'm not going to tell you again. Either you get off my property or I'm calling the police!"

The man was about to call the local police station, but the officials walked toward him and grabbed him. "I guess we're going to do it the hard way," the black official said.

"Get off me! What are you doing?! You can't do this, you crooked bastards!" The black official was getting frustrated and was thinking of a way to subdue the man. Both of the officials were pulling the man as they walked closer to their parked vehicle. The black official took the man's head and bashed it onto the back window of their Mercedes-Benz sedan. It had a silver metallic finish to it with slight modifications. No performance modifications, just exterior. The armored steel plating implanted behind the car's paint was hard enough to temporarily stun the man. The man was now taken as a hostage.

Moments later, the hostage finally wakes up. He's sitting in between the same two men in the back seats of the vehicle. Despite the injuries that the hostage sustained, he surprisingly doesn't stain the black, leather seats. The hostage has a red lump on the right side of his forehead resembling the shape of an oval and the size of a large pin with some lacerations. He also has a noticeable black eye on his right eye. His hands are chained to his back as the chain was silver.

The hostage spoke to the driver and the officials, "Why are you doing this? What do you want from me?" The driver was white in skin color while wearing the same attire as the officials.

"Please, sir. I don't need your questions for the answers you want. Your time's up, so stop talking and sit tight. Make yourself comfortable if you can," the driver said.

"So it is true. You're responsible for all those deaths. I knew all of you were crooked-"

"Enough! I said no talking! Keep it up or we'll kill you right now!"

The hostage was about to leap over the driver's seat. The driver became alert, "Agents, subdue him!" The agents started to repeatedly punch the hostage mostly in the chestal region. The hostage was starting to get bruised to the extent that created the sensory illusion of broken ribs. His diaphragm was being heavily beaten, causing a shortness of breath in a matter of seconds.

After the beating was over, the hostage was coughing so much that blood came out of his mouth and left a stain on the carpet floor. The driver spoke once more, "Agents, that's enough. Let him catch his breath. Save the rest for later." The beaten hostage was about to speak, but his voice sounded weak, "You'll go to hell..... for this. Just you...... wait."

Two hours later, the agents arrive at their destination. There was barb fencing with two gate doors in the middle.

There is a parking lot that's mostly filled with vehicles.

They're beside a gray building that was just recently built as it

was white and showed no signs of aging. It is about the size of

an average capital city building. There was an insignia that's

located just below the top of the building that's similar to

what a person would see on a traditional governmental

facility. It looks more like the symbol of the Federal Bureau of

Investigation.

The driver abruptly stopped the vehicle and opened his

car door. He ran to the gate doors and started to spin the

dials on a combination lock in the middle of the doors. After

he unlocked them, he violently pushed them open and ran

back to the vehicle. He then drove into the middle of the

parking lot. After he put the vehicle in park and shut it off, the

agents opened their doors. The black agent pulled the

hostage out. The white agent walked around the front

bumper of the sedan.

The agents escort the hostage to the silver-colored,

security-activated, steel double doors, which are ten feet high and twenty feet wide. The driver put the vehicle in reverse and turned to the right to face the road. He drove to the edge of the parking lot and immediately turned left. He propelled off into the road with brutal acceleration and left the gate doors open.

The white agent entered in a twenty number combination on the neon green touchscreen security lock beside the doors. The display had the same layout as a telephone. The access was denied, which confused the agents for a moment. The white agent realized he made a mistype on the lock. The black agent got frustrated as he pushed the white agent and hostage aside as they collapsed to the ground. "Move aside, I'll do it! We don't have time for this!" the black agent yelled. He managed to enter the combination without any flaws. The security doors opened as the agents waited. The white agent got up on his feet.

Both of the agents walked to the hostage and pulled him up with aggressive force and pushed him into the entrance hallway. The halls were dim, but visible enough without the use of flashlights. The ceiling lights emitted a tannish color. The hostage started to tear up from the pain.

As the agents approach the twin doors ahead of them, they think about barging through them. The agents are pulling the hostage harder, but are struggling as he is dragging. The agents move with more speed. They are pulling with more effort as they head for the double doors, which are at least thirty feet away.

The agents approach the doors and barged through with heavy force and entered another hallway. The hallway they entered in was different from the other one as it has more lights, making it white all across it. It splits in both directions with another hallway, presenting a long straight in the center.

The agents take a left as they approach another door as it also had a digital security lock. Its display by the right side of the door was red with the same layout as the double doors from outside. Almost every door inside and out of the building has a security lock to prevent other "subjects" like the hostage from escaping. The white agent types in the combination with no problem. They open the door to reveal a dark room and violently pushed the hostage into it. The push knocked the hostage out cold after sustaining multiple injuries.

After a long while, the hostage wakes up, dazed and confused, in the same room except it was lit up in the center with a light protruding from the ceiling. He's sitting in front of a gray table while still feeling whiplash from earlier in the day. His arms and legs are strapped to a chair as he couldn't move, but was too weak to even try. After the man recollects himself, he looks around and spots the agents standing in front of him. "So, sir. How do you feel?" the black agent said with a cunning and sarcastic voice. The hostage spoke while trying to breathe, "You make me sick. You still didn't explain yourselves. You don't have the cojones to do so."

The black agent was pacing calmly, "We are a top-secret organization that no one knows our true identity. We're going to ask you a few questions before we move on to the next step." He speaks in a more serious tone, "So tell me, how do you know about the organization?"

The hostage spoke in a stronger tone, but still struggles to keep himself stable, "I don't know you people personally, but I have a good idea of why all of these people are randomly disappearing. It's on the media. Everyone knows about the disappearances. You're the people behind all of-"

"That's enough, sir. You've said what you had to say," the black agent interrupted. The hostage raises his voice a little more than last time, showing anger and impatience, "I'm not finished yet. You can't even let me finish my answer. You can't even answer *my* questions I asked you earlier. Never really thought that "government officials" were so cowardly!" The black agent got frustrated and lost his patience, "That's it! It's time to put you down!" The black agent gave the other agent an order, "On to the next step of the termination process."

The white agent had a pistol in his pocket that's similar to the appearance of a Browning 9mm handgun. The gun is black as the barrel was silver like other traditional handguns. He loads the magazine until it's in its full capacity. He cocks the gun to prepare for the next step. The hostage makes another remark to the black agent, "*Tst*. It's a damn shame. Making other people do all the dirty work for you. I see who you really are now."

The black agent makes a statement to the hostage while the other awaits the next step, "You may got spunk and I find that intriguing." The black agent walks up to the hostage and takes his hand to grab his neck with a firm grip. He's now speaking in an aggressive tone, "But I'll make this clear right now. We will stop at nothing until we kill the person with the next number. Everyone has one, but they expect nothing of it. No matter how much it's been circulated, no matter how many rumors were spread, they will expect nothing! Just face it, your number's up!" The black agent speaks to the other agent, "Please, continue the termination process."

The white agent walks toward the hostage. The black agent says, "That's the way we do things around here." The white agent slowly raises the pistol. The hostage screams in panic, "No, wait, what are you doing?!! Please stop!" The hostage speaks with a softer, yet horrified tone while tearing up from the pressure, "What do you want from me? What did I ever do to you? Just please answer those questions, that's all I'm asking!" The pistol is drawn closer to his forehead. The black agent says, "I'm sorry it has to be this way. It's part of life. You should learn that by now." The hostage says his last words in anger and agony, "Go to hell, you son of a bitch!"

The gun is pointing a few inches away from the hostage's forehead. He looked through the silver barrel of the pistol and closed his eyes as he was shaking to the extent of a skipping heartbeat. The white agent slowly pulled the trigger as the bullet came out with intense velocity. It traveled through his forehead and exited through the rear towards the center part of his skull. The hostage jerked himself backwards from the impact as he showed no signs of life. The agents paused for a moment.

The black agent turned the light switch off of the interrogation room and walked towards the double doors. The agents opened the doors and walked into the hallway as the doors closed behind the deceased man.

THE NUMBER CONSPIRACY

Chapter 1: Prosperity

July 20, 2019

In the urban districts of New York City, the tall skyscrapers and the welcoming sun at midday, brings the common factors of a luxury that anyone can afford in an average daily lifestyle. The economy has made an effort to keep up with stability for a wealthier society. The economic status was in a such established condition, prosperity wasn't as big of a surprise that many thought it would be. People managed to keep up with their bills as soon as they got informed of them. The skyscrapers were made with better material for improved stability and efficiency. The transportation choices are no longer uncommon. The vehicles

that were once a common sight, such as a Ford Focus, have

become a rarity. The vehicles are now mostly sports cars and

vehicles that are high in performance, such as a Jaguar XK

and a Lamborghini Aventador, which both originate from

European countries. A person would be lucky if they saw a

Chevrolet Cruze anywhere. One of the only classes of vehicles

that managed to survive were trucks. Trucks managed to keep

their name alive due to their durability. The environmental

status has made some progress as well. The Environmental

Protection Agency has approved some countries to be clean

that once had high levels of pollution.

It starts off with a man named Darrell Friegman, who's

walking down the sidewalk of a busy street in deep city

territory. He's white in skin color with black hair, wearing a

black shirt, blue denim jeans and Starter brand tennis shoes.

He was carrying a black, three-foot, cylindrical office

equipment bag with the strap over his shoulder. As he was

walking to the tall buildings in front of him, he looked around to see people talking to each other, but walked on, minding his own business.

Darrell kept walking until he saw a newspaper stand. The headline reads "MAN MYSTERIOUSLY DISAPPEARS WITHOUT A TRACE" with the picture of a man appearing to be of foreign descent. As he skimmered through the newspaper, he quickly got back into reading the main article of the headline.

The caption stated, "Last seen July 19, 2019. The man had black hair and appeared to be of Mexican descent. Skin is slightly tan. He was wearing a white dress shirt with a black tie, dress pants and shoes. Witnesses say that the man appeared to be interrogated by two men near his front door, white and black in skin color while appearing to be from a business company. There was a Mercedes-Benz sedan parked by the man's house at the time of the incident. Witnesses spotted the men in black taking the man by force and bashing his forehead on the passenger door. The impact was heavy enough to leave a bloodstain near the man's driveway. Investigations of the incident are still underway. Further information will be given whenever possible."

"Hmm.....another one missing already," Darrell said to himself. He's used to this kind of news. Nothing really seemed to surprise him anymore. This was a recent, yet common problem in the society that people including Darrell know of today. This didn't start happening until a couple years back. There was a mixed reaction with people. Some were confused and worrisome while others were skeptical and just carried on with their lives. There was a rumor going on about an organization that's involved in organized crime. The description of the people affiliated within the organization usually wore formal clothes mostly in black. Most of the members of the organization wear sunglasses. They'll use anything that stands out. They'll do anything to get the job done. Once the rumor started circulating, it started to become a conspiracy. The conspiracy was that everyone had their own unique number imprinted in their body called cancellation numbers. The legend of the conspiracy is that sometimes when you see men dressed in black, that means your number is next, which also means you're dead. People really couldn't do anything about it.

Darrell stopped reading and continued walking in the same direction from earlier. "I wonder if it's all true," he said. He kept walking until he reached the parking lot of his workplace. He worked in the financial department. He walked in the walking area of the parking lot of Parking Garage B, which was out of two parking garages next to each other. After walking in the lot, he entered the parking garage. The garage was well lit on the inside like it was nighttime. The lights were visible as he walked every few feet. They were orange-yellow in color to mimic the ambience of nighttime. The garage had thirty-three floors with each floor fitting at least two hundred vehicles. His vehicle was parked on the eighth floor. He owned a Volvo sedan, which is yellow and had chrome alloy rims with LED headlights and taillights. Vehicles were getting more detailed by the exterior and interior features in the automobile industry.

Darrell was on the eighth floor as he saw at least forty

parked vehicles. There are ten lanes on each floor to provide enough room for workers to enter and leave the building. His Volvo is located to the far right side of the floor. He walked to his car and opened the door.

While Darrell was checking for his keys, he checked his cell phone for recent messages. He had no other messages besides the ones from his boss praising him for his performance at work. He gets in his car and closes the door. He pulls the seat belt down until it clicks to his side. He puts his keys in the ignition to start the engine. Darrell checks for vehicles and exits while maintaining the garage's speed limit of ten miles per hour.

After driving down several floors, Darrell exits the lot and drives on the road. He accelerates to forty-five miles per hour, quickly shifting to second gear. He reached that speed limit at around five to six seconds. He was alert, but calm as he was driving through the long and busy roads of New York City.

As the day approached sunset, Darrell was just a couple miles away from his home in the suburbs. It was dark enough for him to turn on the lights in his car. He lives in a quiet

neighborhood.

The interior was incredibly advanced in technology. It is a

model year car, too. The gauges were all digital in ocean blue.

The center of the dashboard had a highly advanced

navigation system, so advanced that it was hard for the

leading brand to keep up. The global positioning system was

getting better with accuracy of calculating directions. There

aren't many buttons by the GPS. The only buttons were the

air conditioning, ranging from sixty to eighty degrees

Fahrenheit, but they were touch sensitive. There were

different options for driving because of the higher demand of

people asking for choices of the way people drive.

In Darrell's car, the driving modes are Cruise, Sport, Sport

Plus, and Economy. His car is in Cruise mode. He was going

fifty miles per hour on the road he was on, which was a mile

and a half long. As he's about to reach the end of the road, he

sees a stop sign to patiently wait for oncoming vehicles, but

no vehicles were coming.

Darrell makes a right to find his way to a road full of houses. He kept his vehicle going until he reached his house. His house was located on the right side of the road. His driveway was longer than the other houses on his block and was wide enough to fit two vehicles at one time. His house consisted of two floors. It was white on the outside with a garage located by the side of his house. He parked his vehicle into the garage. He exited his car and walked up the porch towards his front door.

Darrell opens the front door to his kitchen. Same with the exterior, his kitchen is colored in brilliant white. There was a sink located on the side of the kitchen as there was a dining table located in the center. The sink's knobs were chrome in color as the dining table was white, but had steel accented chairs to mimic the workstation of an office.

Darrell sets his equipment bag on the table to unpack. He breathes calmly as he takes out his office papers out of one of the zipping compartments. He pauses to think about the news article from earlier. He kept unpacking until his bag was empty.

Darrell took all of his equipment and walked upstairs. The stairs crossed from right to left in a short spiral as he walked up to the second floor. The rooms were arranged from right to left. The floor had a bathroom, a closet, a laundry room, and finally, his bedroom. Darrell walked down the hallway as there was a small dim ceiling light that's lit across the right side. The floors were made of arched earlywood and latewood tiles.

Darrell continued to walk until he reached the white bathroom door. The walls were white along with its linoleum floor tiles. There was a white shower cabinet towards the right side of the bathroom along with a white bathtub with curtains in the far center. He opened the cupboard just under the sink by the other side of the bathtub to find his toothbrush. His toothbrush was white with red accents.

Darrell looked himself in the mirror to see he was very tired. It was a long day for him. After reading the article and a busy day at work, he was a little worn out for the night. He noticed the fatigue in his eyes. It was around nine o'clock at the time. He woke himself as he squeezed toothpaste out of the tube and started brushing his teeth. He was rhythmically brushing his molars, incisors, and lastly his tongue. It didn't take more than a minute and a half until he was done. He rinsed his mouth out with water and turned off the light switch in the bathroom.

Darrell went back into the hallway to go to his bedroom to see the dark brown walls. The room's environment is more relaxing than the other rooms in his house. His bed is on one side of the room while the television on his dresser is across from his bed, giving him space to walk freely. He turned on a lamp by his bed to see more of his room.

Darrell walked up to his dresser and opened the top drawer as he changes his clothes to get ready for bed. He put on red pajamas and a white T-shirt to make him more comfortable. Just before he was about to lay down, he put on some Axe brand deodorant and checked his phone. He unlocked the screen to see that it was ten minutes past nine.

He has to be at work by six-thirty in the morning. He walks to his bed to fix his sheets and lays down to call it a night. As he's in bed, he turns off the light switch of a lamp on a small cupboard by his side. The room was pitch black as it made it comfortable for him to sleep. He made a big sigh and closed his eyes to prepare himself for another day of work ahead of him.

Chapter 2: Flashbacks

July 19, 2019

The agents walked away from the doors as the man lays with no movement. The agents walked at a calmer pace. "You need to act tougher than you did back there," said the black agent. The black agent's name was Barrett Atkinson. He was muscular in body shape. He also had black hair that looked like it was just starting to grow back. He's usually the guy that pushes people to do harsh things.

The other agent was Warren Leyton. He's the guy that does anything he's told, but has a habit of thinking about an event after a certain occurrence. "I shot the guy in cold blood, what more do you want?" Warren said.

"Listen to what you're saying. The way you were holding that gun. Oh, man, you were shaking like it was winter outside, but I'll cut you some slack since you're new to this." Warren always had to play innocent every time he regrets doing something. He's one of the more sensitive kinds of people that get emotional and this was one of the times to do so. He always tried to keep his emotions to himself. If Barrett sees him choke up while on the job, Leyton would never see the light of day again.

It all happened two years ago on July of 2017. Warren started to change the way he thinks about the outside world. He was twenty-four years old at the time. He became more careless to anyone around him, but that wasn't the worst of it. He had a very grand life. He had a beautiful wife with blonde hair and blue eyes that could mystify anyone. He was working in the same company as Darrell was. He used to make excellent pay, he brought home about $2,500 a week, but wasn't always placed in the right situations.

It traces back to Warren's childhood. His father, Johnathon was working for an organized crime syndicate back in 2001 when he was just eight years old. His father was wanted for seventeen counts of murder, car theft, and conspiracy. His mother, Elaine worked in a car theft syndicate, which made her wanted not only for car theft, but also in numerous hot pursuits by police authority. This made her No. 8 on the FBI's Most Wanted list.

When Warren was fourteen years old, his behavior and self-esteem deteriorated and changed his views on society. He was physically abused regularly by his father. He often got punched and bruised if he didn't do what he was told. He wasn't fond of what his father was doing.

The event took place in the kitchen. The walls were tan. Johnathon was sitting on an old, black chair while near a table that's light blue. Warren's father had long hair that was black. He was standing a few feet from his father while trying to confront him. "Dad, you know you don't have to live this way. Murder is never the answer!" Warren yelled.

"Warren, this is what I do! I'm doing it for our family! We don't have the time or money to just relax and think everything's going to be alright! You should've learned that by now!"

"Yeah, but YOU could do other things instead of killing people for no reason besides their damn money! What kind of father figure are you?!" Johnathon snapped when his son talked back at him, "WARREN! Don't you dare talk back at me! You better shape up your attitude or your ass is going to be beat, mister!" Warren was crying at this point. Warren said, "Yeah, like you always do to Mom! She's not perfect, either, but you're sick, dude. I don't even want to be around you both! BOTH of you were never good parents!"

"THAT'S IT!" Johnathon angrily stormed out of his chair and grabbed his son by the hair. Warren's hair was longer than what it was in present day. The length of his hair at the time was long enough to touch just above his eyebrows. His father shoved him into his room onto the wooden part of his bed and started beating him. Fists were flying left and right.

Warren was beaten up to the point that he was bruised. The beating lasted for twenty seconds.

After the malicious beating, Warren's father crouched down to where he was sitting. He was feeling weak as his father looked angrily at him, dead in the eye. Johnathon got up and stormed out of his room. Warren's chest was heavily bruised while his face was slightly bloodied and got a black eye. He laid down on the floor and cried even more. He wasn't crying just because of the physical pain, but also because he felt so heartbroken by his father that he would senselessly beat his own son. His view on people and society changed since that incident.

When Warren was nineteen, he got approved for a job at B&N Financing. He was gifted for his smarts at school when it came to finances. He was working as an employee within the marketing campaign of the company as he was pulling in about $1,500 a week as his starting salary.

Warren was standing in the middle of the lobby room, carrying an office equipment bag with the strap over his shoulder. He was wearing formal attire in all black except for his white dress shirt and was wearing a black tie. The lobby was mostly surrounded by windows as walls on one side. There was a wooden clipboard with papers on the counter of the lobby booth next to the glass entrance doors. There were a couple escalators with the exception of a couple elevators. Many people were walking around as there were hundreds.

It wasn't long when Warren spotted a seemingly attractive woman happily smiling and talking to the lobbyist while signing in for work. Her name was Phoenix Hadaway. Her skin was white in color as it was clean in texture. Her hair was the finest shade of blonde that would make anyone want her and had blue eyes that reflected like crystals. Her body was thin as her arms and legs were slender. She was about six feet tall. She wore a white shirt, bearing the company's name with blue jeans and white tennis shoes. Warren looked at her for a few seconds, but without hesitation, he walked over to greet her.

As Warren was ten feet away from Phoenix, she

accidentally dropped her paperwork on the floor. She had a manila folder that was almost full of it. He stopped walking as he's about to help pick up her paperwork. "Here, let me help you with that," Warren said. She was in shock, but kept her feelings to herself.

"It's cool, I got it," Phoenix said.

"You sure? You got a lot of papers in that folder."

"Yeah, I'm good, but thank you though."

Phoenix nervously looked at Warren and walked away. He was checking if she was missing anything. She was missing her application form. Warren quickly picked it up from the floor and ran towards Phoenix. "Hey, ma'am! Ma'am!" he said. Phoenix was shocked yet again. "Did you forget this?"

Phoenix was in question as she thought that Warren was trying to flirt with her, but noticed her application form in his hand. "Oh, thank you, sir. That was nice of you. I would've been screwed without it," she said in relief.

"No problem." Phoenix gave Warren a smile, but was still confused of why he was nice to her on her first day there.

After a few moments, she turned away and continued

walking. She reached the waiting area on the far side of the

lobby room. The waiting area was a few hundred feet away

from where he was standing.

Warren was still standing in the same spot as he was

hesitant. He went to the silver, metallic elevator that's located

just a few feet away from the booth. He waited patiently for

the elevator to descend due to the massive number of office

rooms on each floor.

The light pointing downward above the elevator doors

started to flash red. The doors opened. Six people came out,

but weren't in a hurry. Warren didn't personally know the

people, but noticed it was the end of their shift for the day.

The people were signing out on the sign-in forms on the

lobby counter. Warren pressed the UP button on the bottom

of the screen of the touch sensitive pad to keep the doors

open. He entered the elevator and turned around to swipe

his finger up until the number, 8 displayed on the touchpad.

The screen had all of the numbers of the floors that ranged

from 1 to 33. The elevator has a relatively, luxurious feel to it. The interior had a brown, wooden finish with mirrors on the back wall. The elevator has two lights shining brilliantly from its ceiling. Above the elevator doors were arrows facing opposite directions from each other.

As the elevator ascended, Warren turned around to face the mirrored wall. He gave a quick look at himself, showing confidence and giving a vigorous smile. He made a big, relaxing sigh to keep himself focused while preparing for work. The elevator showed that he just passed the fifth floor on the red digital display above the doors.

The elevator reached the eighth floor. Warren was greeted by the silver, metallic walls of the corridors and hallways. He walked to his left and made another left to view two offices with partially mirrored walls on one side of the hallway. He noticed that each of the windows on the other side of the hallway were about five feet high and ten feet apart, projecting the flawless blue skies outside. While walking, he saw a couple bushes in vases on one side of the hallway. The hallways were well lit as he continued walking in the light gray corridors.

As soon as Warren reached the end of the hallway, he entered another. This time, it was lit with a slight tint of yellow from the sun. He stopped to open the door of Office No. 835.

Warren walked in to view the brilliant white walls with a seven-foot marble desk in the center of his office. He set his equipment bag down by the side of the door and sits in the black office chair in front of the desk. The office room shined brightly from the windows behind it. Instead of a traditional computer keyboard, there was a holographic keyboard below a fifteen-inch, digital touchscreen interface.

Warren turned on the computer's server with the hand scanner by the interface. The computer was operating at a relatively fast speed. He patiently waited until the interface brought up the login window. He typed in his username and password.

Warren successfully logs in as he sees the screen's

wallpaper. The interface's wallpaper was traditional, as it bears his company's name. The display of the interface was green in the middle as there was a small red display on the bottom right side. The red display represented references, such as the current time and the date while the green display represented the overall interface for the applications. He swiped his hand to the left of the interface to view the icon of an office application.

After Warren opened the application, the black office phone towards the door started ringing. The phone was wireless with a touch sensitive numeric pad below it. The phone had only two buttons, which were the SPEAKER and TALK buttons. It was being supported by a black small charging station just above the touchpad. He immediately stood up and walked to the phone. The phone rang two times before he could pick it up and puts it to his ear, "Hello?" It was the chief executive officer of B&N Financing, which was a male, "You've been scheduled for an early shift throughout the week."

"I already knew that. Thanks for the heads up."

"Bye." Warren was working for B&N Financing for about a year to know and keep track of his schedule. His current week's shift was from seven o'clock in the morning to one o'clock in the afternoon. After he got off the phone, Warren looked down on his silver diamond watch around his wrist to check the time. He was shocked that he barely got any work done and it was already nine o'clock.

Warren sat back down and started typing away in the office application. It was for promoting the company's name. He also has some programming skills as well. People never really knew the backstory of his life. He has been keeping his past to himself for a very long time. He was thinking about his childhood, which made him perform a typo. He paused for a moment. He made a sigh of tension and returned to typing.

Warren was redesigning the brochures. The brochures had a formal, yet friendly setting in the few pages of each of them. It talked about the company's history, the jobs and duties, and the average salaries. The company was fairly old as it was established in 1993, which was the same year of

Warren's birth. He was given one of the better salaries, which

was around $60,000 to $100,000 a year. His mood was

uplifted as he was typing about the marketing campaign and

the other jobs and duties. The brochure was bigger than

traditional size as it was twelve inches wide and nine inches

tall.

As Warren was nearing the end of the second page, the

speaker above the doors of his office beeped repeatedly. He

was a bit startled as he was still focused on the brochure. He

looked down at his watch to see that it was ten o'clock. "Ooh!

Lunch break," Warren excitedly whispered.

Warren quickly stood up and walked to his equipment

bag. It was black with blue, striped accents in the center

while bearing the company's name in the center as well. He

crouched down and unzipped the front compartment to grab

his lunchbox. His lunchbox is also black with gray, red, and

green accents ringed around to its top with the colors from

top to bottom. The lunchbox was big in size, too as it was

about fifteen inches wide and a foot in height.

Warren got up and stretched for a few seconds after a hard hour's work. He opened his office door to promenade in the opposite directions leading from his office. He sees a hallway full of employees on their way to lunch. The overall light of the hallways have somewhat changed as it was brighter. The hallways were cooler in temperature. He felt relaxed from the atmosphere around him. In the middle of the hallway, he coughed, but wasn't a sign of sickness. He always liked to look around as he made a couple glimpses from left to right.

As he reached the end, Warren noticed the elevator stations in the center being lit by the sun. There's five elevators on both sides. The elevator doors were silver and had silver touch-sensitive numeric pads next to them with orange LED displays. He faced the same elevator from earlier. He tapped the arrow pointing down on the touchpad and waited patiently for it to open. A small square on the bottom blinked the color of neon green.

The arrow pointing down flashed red. The elevator opened to greet Warren into its luxurious interior. The brown, wooden, stained walls were reflecting their shine.

Warren turned around to face the elevators on the opposite side. He swiped down until the touchpad viewed the number, 1, indicating the first floor and the elevator closed.

Warren turned around to face the mirrored wall to check if he missed anything from earlier. There was a couple strands of his hair on his shoulder. He quickly brushed it off with his arm as if it wasn't even there in the first place. He turned around to face the elevator doors. He sighed to release some stress to prepare himself for lunch. The touchpad displayed that he's now on the first floor.

The elevator opened as the sun's rays from the windows shined in the elevator room. He walked out and turned right to view the lobby. People were walking in all directions as most of the employees were heading to the cafeteria. The cafeteria was distantly located to the far side of the lobby. Some employees still had work during this time of day. He slowly walked to the cafeteria as the sun glared behind him.

Warren arrived a moment too late as the lunch line was nearly full in front of the silver, metallic entrance doors to the cafeteria. The line made a twenty-foot distance from the doors. He wasn't surprised that the line was this long by the time he arrived. He walked to the last of twenty people in line. The man in front of him had black hair while wearing a black T-shirt, bearing the company's name and wearing Starter brand tennis shoes. It was Darrell Friegman, but Warren didn't recognize him in any way.

Darrell looked behind him to see that Warren was there, but they didn't talk. His eyes were caught off guard as Darrell looked at him. They both made direct eye contact for a couple seconds. Darrell turned back around to face the cafeteria.

After ten minutes, the line shortened to the point that Warren spotted the cafeteria's interior. The ceiling lights were dimly lit. The sunlight from the windows were the main source of light. There was a guardrail that was a continuation of the line. He walked to his right and followed the guardrail. While he was standing between the guardrail, he saw another part of the lunch line going to the left and noticed a brightly lit kitchen. There were a couple small steps on both ends of the line.

Warren immediately walked down the small steps since he packed a lunch. There are ten tables that are each able to fit at least a hundred people. He walked to the table that was located third to the left side and took a seat by the windows. The sunlight was glaring on the floor next to where he is sitting.

Warren unzipped his lunchbox and took out its contents. Everything in his lunchbox were all enclosed by sandwich bags that were all airtight for maximum freshness. He had a bologna sandwich topped with pepper jack and cheddar cheese with lettuce and sliced chip-chopped ham with a sesame seed bun. He had two water bottles that were shivery to the touch. He also has another sandwich containing deli chicken seasoned with Cajun and deli turkey with cheddar and mozzarella cheese topped with lettuce along with a sesame seed bun.

As Warren took a bite out of his bologna sandwich, he spotted Phoenix in line getting her lunch. He was hesitant while looking at her, but quickly resumed looking at his sandwich. Her dish was full and ready to eat. She was about to make a vanilla coffee latte out of the coffee machine, which was near the end of the line. She inserted a one-dollar bill into the machine to pay for her coffee.

After Phoenix fixed her lunch, she walked down the small steps as the sunlight glared onto her body. She was confused as she was walking around for a place to sit. She was a few tables from Warren. After roaming, she spotted him sitting alone while eating his bologna sandwich. They locked eyes for a few seconds until she was convinced and walked to his point of view. Phoenix walked from the table she was at and smiled at him. "I don't really have anywhere to sit, so I might as well sit with you," she said as she sat from the other side of him.

"Go ahead."

Warren and Phoenix were sitting face to face. She had all of the menu contents on her tray for the day's lunch. There were cheesy green beans, a pork chop, a peach, and a bottle of water accompanied by silverware, which contained a fork, a spoon, a knife and some napkins. She picked up her knife and starting cutting into her pork chop. She pierced the cleaved piece. She started chewing and swallowed it. "They make some pretty good food here," she said.

"Tell me about it. You'll get used to it the more you come here." Phoenix laughed after he spoke. "By the way, thanks for helping me with my paperwork earlier, but, really, you didn't have to do that," she said.

"There's thousands of people that work here. I couldn't let you be late on your first day. Who else was going to help you?" Warren finished his bologna sandwich. Phoenix was hesitant, "But again thanks, that was nice of you."

"No problem."

"How long have you been working here?"

"For about a year. How do you like your first day here?"

"Oh, I love it here. It's clean, organized, and it's pretty high-tech here."

"Yeah, but not to mention that the economy nowadays hasn't been that great," Warren said. Phoenix chuckled, "You got that right. I was lucky to get a job here knowing that I have a college degree in business."

"Is this your first job?"

"Yes it is." They paused to finish their lunches.

Warren and Phoenix got up and walked to the small steps near the coffee machine. They were standing beside each other while Phoenix was holding her tray and Warren was carrying his sandwich bags. She set her tray on a counter from the left side of the kitchen. He threw away his sandwich bags in a garbage can by the coffee machine. They turned around and walked down the small steps. "You seem like a nice woman, what's your name?" Warren said.

"My name's Phoenix. Phoenix Hadaway."

"Name's Warren Leyton."

"Nice to meet you, Warren." They kept walking until they sat back down.

"You know what, Warren? I want to get to know you more," Phoenix said curiously. He wasn't expecting an answer like that. Warren was shocked, "Wh-what? Are you serious?" Phoenix folded her arms on the table and moved her upper body closer to Warren. She raised one of her eyebrows to show that she wasn't joking. She was still smiling, but was acting more serious than earlier and showed her flirtatious side. She politely insisted, "Now do you think I would be kidding? I want to get to know you. You seem like a nice guy." Warren chuckled in disbelief. He never had a chance like this before. It seemed like all of a sudden some weight has been lifted off of him. He started to show his lighter side. "Uh...I honestly don't know what to say. I don't know what to think," he said. Phoenix kept her smile and locked her eyes with him. She lifted her arms up and locked her hands together under her chin. She now has her elbows on the table.

Phoenix noticed a tear drop from Warren's eye. Her

smile dropped as she showed sympathy towards him. She said collectedly, "Aww, I didn't mean to make you cry, Warren."

"Oh, no, no, no, it's not you, Phoenix."

"What's the matter, Warren? Is there something you want to talk about?" He shed a couple more tears, but kept himself from making a scene. "You don't even know how much this means to me right now. There's so much to talk about, it's not even funny, literally," he paused. "You're one of the only people that's actually showed a sign of caring towards me. The funny thing is, I've only known you for about twenty minutes. There wasn't anyone this caring enough around me."

"Warren, please don't cry. I can tell that there's something terribly wrong. You can trust me, you can talk to me about anything." He teared up more as he thought about his childhood. Phoenix pleaded, "It's alright, Warren. Just talk to me, be open."

Warren quietly sighed to put himself in control of his

emotions, "Alright." He hesitated before continuing. Phoenix was paying close attention to what he had to say. He said, "My mother and father. They weren't really considered as family to me. My father was working with a gang that involved with theft and killing people. Johnathon Leyton was his name. He was convicted with seventeen counts of murder and the list goes on." Phoenix was shocked.

Warren was starting to reach his breaking point as he teared up more. He felt like yelling and screaming, but kept his emotions to himself. He continues to explain his story, "He didn't give a *damn* about anything. He never was considered as a father figure to me. All he cared about was himself."

Phoenix started to shed a tear as she's feeling the same emotions as Warren. He continued, "I was fourteen at the time. I was forced to accept the lifestyle he was living. I was trying to tell him that he shouldn't be living that way. He never listened to me. He was oblivious to what I had to say. He started yelling and screaming at me, but it didn't end there. He grabbed me and threw me in my room and started beating the hell out of me. I was being punched all around me until I was bleeding and bruised. I was devastated that my father, my *own* father, would do such bodily harm to his own child. He used to abuse my mother as well, but my mother wasn't that great either. She was a thief. She had a really bad habit of stealing cars and getting in trouble with the police. She didn't care about what she was doing, either. She did whatever was on her mind and only cared about herself and whoever she worked with. After that incident with my father, my view on people has changed ever since." Phoenix sheds a couple more tears after Warren explained his childhood experiences, "Oh, that's terrible, Warren! How were you able to go through something like that?"

"I know, I'm surprised he didn't kill me that day. I never had contact with my family ever since."

Phoenix let her arm down to reach out for Warren's arm and show some affection. She said, "I'll tell you this, you know why you're still standing to this day, Warren?"

"Why's that?"

"It's because you're strong. You managed to get up from your feet and do something positive in your life. You decided not to become like them, Warren. What doesn't kill you makes you stronger." Warren nodded, showing that he got the message.

Phoenix said, "You know, I'm glad we talked about this, Warren. When you open up, it lifts a lot of weight off of your shoulders. You'll feel a lot better if you open up about something." Warren laughed in relief and said, "You got that right, Phoenix." Phoenix was smiling happily at him.

"Now just take a nice, deep breath," Phoenix said. Warren inhaled and calmly exhaled all of the stress to get it out of him. "That's it. Now cheer up, buddy. You have to get back to work."

Phoenix took a glance at the digital clock just below the ceiling behind Warren. The clock read as 10:58, which was two minutes until they're dismissed from their lunch hour. The clock was a foot wide and tall as its display was red in color. He looked behind him to look at the clock and looked back at Phoenix and smiled. "Hmm, guess you were right," he said.

"I can tell you're getting better already."

"Yeah, I am feeling better actually."

"See, I told you you would feel better once you open up." Warren smiled at Phoenix as she smiled back.

The bell rang as everyone including Warren and Phoenix stood up from their table. Everyone was walking out towards the entrance doors. They decided to stay for a few minutes while standing face to face. Phoenix wanted to say one more thing before Warren goes back to his office. As he turned his back, she patted him on his shoulder to get his attention. "Hey, Warren," she said. He turned around to face her. "If there's anything else you want to talk about, you can always let me know, okay?"

"Okay, Phoenix." Warren smiled at her one last time, but was hesitant. "Thanks for the help."

"You're welcome, Warren. That's what I'm here for." He smiled and walked up the small steps.

The sun was still shining intensely as its rays lit up the lobby room. There was a countless number of people walking around in the lobby at the time. He walked to the elevator by the lobby's entrance.

Right before Warren pressed the arrow pointing up on the touchpad, he saw Phoenix walking to an elevator from the opposite side of him. She glanced over at Warren, giving him a smile of confidence. He smiled back. They locked eyes for a few seconds. She winked at Warren. Right before the elevator opened on Phoenix, she waved at him, saying goodbye for the day. He kept his smile and waved back. Phoenix walked in the elevator as it closed behind her. Warren entered the elevator. The doors closed before he could feel the elevator ascend.

Warren went the same directions to reach his office. He continued to work on the brochures for new employees in the future.

After Warren finished the brochure with two hours of passing, he vaulted the strap of his equipment bag over his shoulder and walked back into the hallways. He entered the same elevator and descended as he felt relaxed.

The elevator stopped and opened to view the lobby room. The sun was still shining brilliantly on Warren's body as he walked out. He covered his face with his arm just to walk towards the booth.

There was a slightly tanned man behind the booth's counter. The man had black hair as he was wearing a green and white striped shirt, bearing the company's name. "You leaving early today?" said the man.

"Yeah, have an early shift."

"Ah, did you get done with the work you're supposed to today?"

"Yes, I did." The lobbyist working that day was one of the more caring employees. The company has a reputation of good discipline to make sure other employees get their work done so they don't get in trouble. "Well, hey, I have to get going. Can't hang around this place for too long."

"Don't forget to sign yourself out," the lobbyist noted.

Warren took the pen by the clipboard on the right side of the counter. The clipboard was thick with paper as it gets filled every week from all of the employees working in the building. The sheet the clipboard was on was almost full as there were only a few spaces left to fill. Warren took a few seconds to sign his name and the time signing out. He put the pen back once he was done. He walked to the right side of the automatic doors with the word, OUT in green holographic lettering in the center. He had a couple feet left to walk before the door automatically opened.

As Warren walked outside, he immediately felt and smelt the fresh air in the urban landscapes surrounding him. The weather forecasted was fairly comfortable. The clear, blue skies, the bright sun and the eighty degree temperature was the perfect mix to end a busy day at work. Warren was standing on the sidewalk a few feet from his workplace.

While Warren waited to cross the street, he decided to do some sight-seeing to entertain himself. When he was looking straight, there were ten twelve-foot tall maple trees with rich, healthy green leaves. As he was watching the

vehicles pass by, he mostly saw luxury and sports vehicles,

such as a BMW M3, Nissan 370Z, and a Chrysler 200. All of

the vehicles were going the speed limit, which was forty-five

miles per hour. Luxury and sports cars were becoming more

commonplace at the time. As he was looking in both ways, he

caught a glimpse of the city's infrastructure to notice the tall

buildings.

Warren spotted some clearance on the road. He walked

to the other side to reach the maple trees and the sidewalk

beside it. He started walking under the maple trees' shadows

as the sidewalk was filled with people, but wasn't crowding.

As Warren walked to the end of the line of trees, he saw

the two parking garage buildings for B&N Financing. They

were tan in color with a white letter on the top of each

building, A and B aligned from left to right. There is a wall

that separates both of the garages. He walked into the

entrance of the lot of Parking Garage A to notice the four

hundred car lot filled halfway, but the vehicles were

scattered. He walked on an upward slant to enter the walking area with a guardrail extending all the way to the garage. After walking up the slant, he turned left and walked straight to reach the other end of the lot.

Warren saw the sign, "Parking Entrance" hanging from the wall of the building's exterior. The sign has a white arrow pointing up that's centered in a dark, gray circle. He walked to the right to view the well lit entrance of the garage. The guardrails inside the garage's walking area are about three and a half feet tall after every few feet of walking as they were slightly slanted upward for about ten feet of walking.

There was the number, 1 and a white arrow pointing upward both centered in a dark, gray circle towards the right side of the wall. The ceiling lights tinted the entrance with a dim white color with the wall paint mimicking the color of cement. Warren walked towards the wall and made two lefts until he walked up the upward slants to reach the first floor.

The first floor is just like the other thirty-two floors of the parking garage. The floors were vast with supporting beams extending to the ceiling. The ceiling lights were emitting their dim white hues. Each of the floors were big enough to hold at least two hundred vehicles. He continued to walk straight until he walked to the left on another ramp to reach the next floor. As he set foot on the ramp, he saw the wall with the number, 1 with an arrow pointing down on the right side and the number, 2 on the other side, pointing an arrow upward. The process continued until he reached the third floor.

As Warren saw the entrance sign above him, the floor was already full of vehicles as it was hard to locate his own. He was still standing in the walking area and started to look around. The vehicles on the floor ranged from entry-level to mid-level luxury vehicles. He kept walking until he reached the small steps in the center of the walking area onto the parking floor.

Warren started walking towards the third column to the left of the floor in between two support beams. There was nobody on the floor at the time. He gave out a soft, but quick sigh. "Where's my car?" he said. The vehicle he owns is a silver Mercedes-Benz sedan. He had a big taste for luxury vehicles, especially for his. He was walking through the column, but there was no sign of his vehicle. He was confused.

Warren stopped walking to think until he realized he went onto the wrong side of the floor. He continued walking until he got out of the column. He walked to his right and scanned through the columns of vehicles.

Warren saw a vehicle that was similar to his. He was now by the third column of vehicles on the right side. He stopped walking to take a closer look. He moved his head forward and squinted his eyes to get a better sight of the vehicle in the middle of the column. He found out it was his and started walking towards the vehicle.

While Warren was fifty feet away from his vehicle, he pulled his car keys out of his pocket. His keys had a silver power lock switch with the Mercedes-Benz emblem engraved on the back of it. He pressed the button with an image of an unfastened combination lock to unlock the vehicle.

As Warren walked closer, he saw the stylish details of the vehicle's exterior. The steel seven-spoke rims mixed fluently with the side skirts. The silver, metallic paint reflected brilliantly from the ceiling lights surrounding the vehicle. The taillights were curved in shape as the reverse lights were sandwiched between them. The headlights present a remarkable vision of style with additional LED lights on the bottom of the front bumper. They also project an aggressive expression of its overwhelming design and unique personality.

Once Warren was standing next to his vehicle, he opened the back door. The back seats were black and were big enough to fit three people. The interior of the back doors are also black, and had chrome, door latches on their panels. He took the strap of his equipment bag off of his shoulder and placed it on the seats. After he closed the door, he walked to the driver's door and opened it. He climbed himself into the seat.

The interior in front of the driver and passenger seat was

luxurious in style. Above the center console was the infotainment system. It was an eight inch touchscreen display. The only buttons of choice around the infotainment system were the driving settings by the center console. Different ranges of settings were growing in demand at this time. Same as Darrell's vehicle, the driving settings were Cruise, Sport, Sport Plus, and Economy with the buttons aligning from top to bottom.

Warren buckled his seat belt and started his vehicle. The meters and exterior lights lit up after he turned the key. The interior lights flickered as he turned the key further and heard the roar of the engine. The gauges behind the steering wheel weren't all digital, but had an eye-catching appearance. All of the meters had the same color. They were sky blue on the top until they faded down halfway to their bottom. On the speedometer located in the center behind the steering wheel, there was a white needle with a digital display on the bottom right of the gauge. Towards the right of the speedometer was the tachometer. The oil pressure and water gauges were twice as small as the other gauges.

Warren puts his foot on the brake and pulled the transmission into reverse from the center console. He tapped the throttle until he had enough clearance to make a turn. He slowly turned the wheel to the right until he faced the exit sign ahead of him. He stopped and set the vehicle into drive. The car made a purring noise as he slowly drove up to ten miles per hour. He stopped in front of the exit sign to check for oncoming vehicles. He turned left and drove until he reached the slanted ramp going downwards in the parking floor exit. He made a left and another left to see another downward ramp. This process continued until he reached the parking garage exit.

Once Warren went through the exit, he could already see the afternoon skies. The lot was still halfway full from when he drove into the entrance. He stopped to take precaution of any drivers coming his way.

As there were no vehicles coming, Warren turned right and continued driving until there was another change of direction. He made a left and continued driving until he reached the exit.

The roads were more busy as the vehicles were higher in density. Warren patiently waited for the roads to decongest while hearing the purr of his engine. After a few minutes, he turned right. It was a two-lane road as he entered onto the right side with two other lanes on the oncoming side. He was approaching the speed limit, which was forty-five miles per hour. The tall buildings were moving away as he was driving.

Warren continued driving for a couple hundred yards until he stopped at a two-way intersection. He made a right to exit out of the metropolitan area and into the suburbs of New York City.

Chapter 3: Second Chance

April 27, 2012

It was a Friday morning at B&N Financing. Warren did his daily routine, signing in, and ascending to the eighth floor. He was dressed formally as he wore a black suit jacket, white dress shirt, and black dress shoes. He had to work on the new design for the pamphlet handouts for new employees.

Warren opened the door to his office and set his equipment bag down by the door. The sun was shining brilliantly from the windowsills. He walked to his chair and sat down to turn on the interface. He typed in his username and password to log in.

Warren swiped his finger to the right side until there was an icon of an office application in the center of the screen. He tapped the icon to start working on the front cover of the new pamphlet. He tapped the top right side to minimize the application. The applications zoomed in towards the center to present improved navigation for the user. He swiped his hand to the right side two times until he found the application for editing graphics. He tapped his finger to open up the application.

Once the application opened, Warren moved the cursor to the left side to access the shaping tool. The shaping tool menu smoothly rolled down to the bottom of the screen to show the extensive variety of options. Some of the shapes ranged from circles and hexagons to the line tool and the marquee tool. He tapped on the line tool and mixed it with the curving tool to make a custom ampersand. He inserted the ampersand in the top center of the canvas.

Warren moved the cursor to the text tool on the top left side. A menu rolled down with a wide variety of fonts. He started scrolling down to search for ones he could use for the company's name. He was getting frustrated because of the massive number of fonts presented to him. He noticed a font that interested him, which was only halfway down the list. The font had a formal style as he thought it would be fitting for the company's name. He converted his custom ampersand to a raster image and starts typing.

Warren typed the letters, B and N in between the ampersand in capitalized form. He tapped the cursor by the N and pressed Enter and added another space to type in the text box as it aligned in the center. He typed the word, "Financing" in the space below "B&N".

In the center of the canvas, Warren inserted two pictures of employees working to represent the atmosphere of the workplace. The picture on the left center shows a woman with brown, hair while wearing business attire. The woman was smiling jovially while typing on a holographic keyboard by an interface. The picture in the other side shows the building's exterior with the company's name in the middle of the thirty-third floor. Each of the floors had windows with gaps of ten feet between them. There were thirty windows on each floor on the front side of the building. The bottom of the picture showed two healthy trees with one on each side near the bottom with the sunlight glaring back on their evergreen leaves.

For the bottom of the front cover, Warren typed "A Quick Tour For What's Ahead Of You" for the company's slogan. For the finishing touches, he made a rectangular border around it. The border's color was red and was a quarter of an inch thick. He saved the document as "B&N Front Cover (2012 Edition)".

On the top left side, Warren tapped the "File" menu to open a new file. He typed out information of the occupations for the next few pages of the pamphlet. The occupation ranged from marketing to financial aid.

Warren got up and walked to the tan filing cabinets beside the office door. He opened the top drawer of the cabinet to look for previous publications of the pamphlets.

His finger moved across the tabbed manila folders as he could

feel their tabs.

Warren reached the last folder and pulled it out. They

were the pamphlets. He realized the pamphlets in the folder

were the 2010 edition. The pamphlets explained about the

different occupations, but the designs of the pages were

bland. He went back to his desk and set the folder down and

continued working.

Warren tapped the text tool again. He started off with

the first occupation from the 2010 edition, which belonged in

the marketing section. He could do this in minutes since his

specialty lies in that range. He retyped the information about

the marketing occupations, but revised them by adding a few

sentences.

After minutes of typing, Warren realized that he already

typed out four pages. The pamphlet he copied off of was

neither thick nor thin. He skimmered through it and found

thirty-four pages as a result. He was surprised, but continued

to work on the 2012 edition.

After an hour and a half of working, Warren completely revised all of the occupations. He also finished just in time for the bell to ring for lunch. He didn't bring his lunchbox this time. He was in the mood for buying his lunch. He stood up and moved his arms out and bent his back to stretch. He relaxed himself by making a deep breath to calm all of his muscles. He also fixed his necktie as it was slightly crooked off to the side.

Warren exited his office. The hallway's windows were shining brightly from the sun's rays. He was more alert as he was walking faster than when he opened up to Phoenix the day before. He saw the hallways quickly being filled with employees. It was crowded, but there was enough room for at least three steps of walking. He had to slow down to avoid accidentally bumping into people.

Warren was able to squeeze himself out of the hallway towards the elevator station. The sunlight glared on his clothes as it reflected on his golden, blonde hair. He stopped at the same elevator he took the other day.

Warren entered the elevator. He put his hand in the pocket of his suit jacket while the elevator doors closed in front of him. He was constantly tapping his foot while descending to the first floor.

After a minute of passing, the elevator opened, showing the lobby room. Warren walked out to spot the cafeteria from a distance. The people in the lobby room were walking in all directions as it made a scattered pattern. The size of the cafeteria doors were increasing as he walked closer to them. He looked to see the line of people waiting to get their meals as the line was longer from the other day. He stopped walking to see that the line extended to about half the width of the lobby, which is about a hundred yards.

Warren turned his head to get a better view of the back of the line as he spotted Phoenix at the end. Once he locked eyes with her, he saw her smiling at him in a friendly manner and waved. He smiled back and walked to the end of the line. As he reached Phoenix, the thought of a conversation was already underway. Phoenix turned her head around to look at him, "Hey, Warren."

"Hey, how are you doing today?"

"I was about to ask you the same thing." Warren kept his smile as Phoenix was talking to him. "How are you feeling?"

"I'm actually feeling pretty good today." Phoenix's smile became more vibrant. She turned back around to face the cafeteria. They could see the interior as the line grew short after twenty minutes of waiting. After a few more steps of walking, they enter the cafeteria. The five of the ten tables were already getting filled with people as they sat down to eat their meals.

After ten minutes, Phoenix and Warren were halfway to the kitchen counter. They could smell the aroma of the food cooking ahead of them. "The food smells pretty good today," Phoenix said.

"Oh, yeah, it does." The smell of the food was getting stronger as the line was getting shorter. They walked to the left to see the kitchen from an angle. The kitchen was clearly visible as it was well lit from its interior.

Warren and Phoenix noticed a male and a female chef standing in front of the counter. The chefs were handing out two lunch trays to two people in front of them. After a minute of waiting, Phoenix and Warren were next. They were standing face to face with the chefs. The male chef has a medium build and was the average height. His height was six feet tall and was tan in skin color and had black hair. Both chefs wore black shirts with white aprons, bearing the company's name over the top of their shirts. The female chef has red hair. Her skin tone was white and was more slender than the male chef and half of a foot shorter.

Warren and Phoenix looked past the chefs to peek through how the lunches were made and delivered so fast. The size of the main kitchen was big enough to fit at least thirty chefs at one time. The walls in the kitchen were cream white. On both sides, they noticed that there were conveyor belts with one on each end. Both conveyor belts stretched up to fifteen feet as they ended to the tip of the counter to carry out numerous trays. The conveyor belts were black and made

out of hardened rubber. They noticed the two separated

kitchens located next to the far ends of the belts. They could

only catch a glimpse of what the small kitchens look like. They

saw that the walls inside of them were pearly white. They

saw a couple chefs on the left side turning netted pans over

in the fryers and stoves.

While Warren and Phoenix were sight-seeing the

kitchen, their trays from the belts caught their attention. The

menu for that day's lunch was similar to what a restaurant

would serve. Steam was flailing up from the food. The items

were crispy, steak cut French fries, a meaty double

cheeseburger with custom toppings of the customer's choice,

barbecue baked beans, a piece of Philly cheesesteak pizza

with garlic seasoning topped with provolone, mozzarella, and

cheddar cheese, and a choice of a bottle of water or milk.

"How are you doing?" said the male chef as he was speaking

to Warren.

"Pretty good, how about yourself?" Warren said.

"Just swell." The male chef made a little chuckle. Warren chuckled back.

"You guys make really good food here," Phoenix said to the female chef.

"Why, thank you!" The female chef smiled. The trays were nearing the counter as the belts moved them across the kitchen. The trays were smoothly set into place on the counter without any mess to clean up.

Warren and Phoenix took out their wallets and skimmered through their bills. Warren had a brown wallet stitched with Italian leather with his credit cards and his thick compartment of bills from his previous paydays. Phoenix had a light blue wallet with a five petal pink flower design. She looked through her bill compartment to find a five-dollar bill. When buying a lunch, the price is always two dollars and fifty cents. Warren took his two one-dollar bills and two quarters while Phoenix took her five-dollar bill and handed the chefs their money. The cash register in front of the female chef opened as she was giving Phoenix her change. They picked up their trays and walked to the water and milk beside the kitchen counter.

"Enjoy your lunch, guys!" the female chef said.

"Thank you!" Warren and Phoenix said. They set their trays on the drink counter and selected a bottle of water. They walked down the small steps and walked straight until they sat at the same table from the day before. "Must be in a restaurant mood today, I guess," Phoenix said.

"Definitely smells like a restaurant, too." Warren took a spoonful of baked beans and inserted it into his mouth. The sun was glaring next to them. He wanted to say something, "Hey, Phoenix, there's something I really want to tell you."

"What's that?"

"Umm......I was thinking......that maybe we can hang out this Saturday and go out to eat somewhere, somewhere fancy." Phoenix gave Warren a surprised look while she picked up one of her fries. She was smiling. She swallowed it and said, "And what do you have in mind?" Warren was hesitant.

"Uhh.....I really don't know to be honest with you. There's so many to choose from-"

"Scratch that." Warren was shocked as Phoenix interrupted him. She pointed her finger up, "Hold that thought."

Warren watched as Phoenix was reaching her hand into her pocket. She was shuffling to get something that appeared to be rectangular in shape. He noticed it was her cell phone. She set her elbow on the table with her phone in her hand. It had a black protective casing with a built-in camera on the back of it. She set her phone down and gave him a flirtatious look. They locked eyes with each other. "Surprise me," Phoenix happily insisted. He was shocked yet again. He was flattered, but was hesitant of what to do next.

"Okay," Warren replied. He knew what Phoenix wanted. She wanted him to put his number into her phone. He couldn't touch the phone as if it was his own.

"What's the matter?" Phoenix said, noticing his hesitation.

"Don't want to peek into your contact list. Don't really know the people on your phone." Phoenix was confused, but realized she forgot to set the screen to "Add Contact".

"Oh, I didn't realize I forgot to do that. I'm sorry about that." Phoenix laughed at herself, but was a good sport about it. She slid her phone close to her and started tapping the screen to set up for adding new contacts. Warren laughed with her and said, "It's okay." She gave her phone back to him. There were three boxes to fill in for setting up a new contact. The boxes were for the person's display name, their home phone number, and for their mobile number. He tapped his fingers on the screen to enter his first and last name and his mobile number. Warren gave her phone back. "Okay, it's settled out," Phoenix said. They locked eyes with each other. They made a smirk and kept them for a few seconds. Phoenix looked at the digital clock. "Oh, look at the time!" she said in surprise.

"What's the matter?"

"We have about twenty minutes left and we barely

touched our trays yet!" Their trays were nearly full of food as they were distracted from their conversation. Phoenix laughed, "I think we should start eating our food now." Warren smiled at her.

"Good point, can't waste good food." They bring their attention back to their trays as the food was starting to lose its steam. They were bringing spoonfuls of the baked beans in their mouths. Warren just opened his bottle of water as it was settling by the edge of the table.

After fifteen minutes, Warren and Phoenix were done eating. They stood up from the table with their trays and walked towards the small steps by the coffee machine.

The same two chefs were just walking towards the counter as Warren and Phoenix set their trays on it. "How was your lunch?" said the male chef.

"Good," Warren and Phoenix said.

"How do you like it here?" the female chef was saying to Phoenix.

"Oh, I love it here, this is actually my first job."

"Good, I'm glad you like it," the female chef said

Warren and Phoenix walked away from the counter and

sit back down. The digital clock displayed that it was five

minutes to eleven o'clock. They look at each other in the

eyes. Warren could see the light reflecting from her ocean

blue eyes as her pupils slightly grew. He could sense what she

was trying to tell him. He was lost in a trance as he was

focused solely on her eyes. They could see a future ahead of

them.

The bell just rang to end their lunch hour, causing

Warren and Phoenix to lose their trains of thought. They got

up and stood face to face. They kept their smiles as they still

locked eyes. "So, I guess I will call you later on this week,"

Warren said.

"Okay, sounds good to me."

"I'll look for somewhere to go if I can."

"Lay it on me when you think of one. I can't wait for

Saturday."

"Same here." Warren and Phoenix started blushing as

their cheeks became red. He looked at the digital clock, "Well, I have to get going. I have to work on the pamphlets for the company."

"Okay, I will talk to you later. Call me when you can."

"I will." Warren turned around and walked to the cafeteria doors.

"Bye!" Phoenix shouted to Warren as he was about to walk up the small steps. He slowly turned around to face her point of view.

"See you later," Warren said. He turned to face the cafeteria doors and went back to his office.

The sun was still shining through the windows as it was reflecting on the floor. As Warren entered his office, he lazily slouched in his chair. He took a minute to stretch his arms and legs out, and resumed to work on the pamphlet. He swiped his finger to the right side of the interface until it viewed the icon for editing graphics. He tapped the icon to reopen the application. He still has everything he typed out from earlier. He skimmered to the last few pages of the 2010 edition and typed out the rest of the occupations to revise them for the next three hours.

The time on the interface read as two o'clock in the afternoon, which gives Warren another hour before he has to go home. He tapped, "File" and then, "Save" at the top of the screen. A window popped up in the center. It was like the same window that popped up in the office application. He tapped the box that said, "File Name" on the top of the window. He gave the file a simple name as he typed in "B & N Financing Pamphlet (2012 Edition)" and tapped "Enter."

To kill the leftover hour Warren has, he was thinking about doing some research about various topics on the Internet. He minimized the graphics editor to view the desktop icons. He swiped his finger to the right until he viewed the Internet application and opened the browser.

As the browser opened, Warren tapped the address bar and typed in "www.google.com". The web site opened fast and responsively after he entered the address. He was searching up topics, such as the economy and the overall status of the United States.

Warren looked down on his diamond watch and noticed it was three o'clock. He quickly closed all of the applications he had opened and tapped the task bar on the bottom left side. The task bar rolled upward to view a roster of options. He tapped the last command on the bottom of the task bar that said, "Shut Down". A window popped up in the center and asked if he wanted to shut down or not. He selected "Yes". The interface powered down as the screen shrank into oblivion.

Warren stood up and grabbed the strap of his equipment bag and placed it around his shoulder. He walked into the hallways as the sunlight was dimmer due to the evening closely approaching. He was showing mild signs of fatigue from all of the work in his office.

There was a pre-evening glow in the lobby. The sunlight made the floors look like they were tan in color. He stepped out and walked straight to the lobby booth as people were gathering around to sign themselves out. Today, there was a woman who was standing behind the counter. She was white in skin color and has black hair with a white shirt, bearing the company's name. Her body shape was that of a medium build. "Hi," said the woman in a kind and joyful voice.

"Hey, how are you?" Warren said.

"I'm good, how about yourself?"

"Good." Warren was standing at the center of the counter as he was signing out on the clipboard. He set down the pen in a quick and abrupt way. "You have a good day," he said in a rush.

"Thanks, you too!" Warren quickly traipsed to the automatic doors and captured the blue skies outside. The temperature for the day's weather was satisfying as it was in the mid-seventies. He was waiting to cross as the vehicles passed by.

About thirty seconds have passed as the roads were spacious enough for Warren to cross. After he crossed, he turned left and walked to the guardrail of the entrance of the lot of Parking Garage A.

Warren walked up the slant to see the lights from the ceiling shine down on the floors like new. The third floor had some people in it this time, but the vehicle count wasn't as dense from the day before. He walked down the steps by the center of the guardrail. His car was located next to the floor's exit.

Warren walked to his car. He took the strap off from his equipment bag and set it on the seats. He walked to the driver's side and opened the door. He climbed into the seat and starts the vehicle. Warren set the vehicle in reverse and started driving out of the garage.

Warren maintained his speed as he was driving through the parking garage exit. He stopped to see that two drivers in an orange Dodge sedan and a red Audi coupe are driving towards the exit and are about a hundred yards away from him. He turned right as it was clear to go. He looked in the rear-view mirror to see the vehicles driving behind him as they were under a couple tall maple trees. He couldn't tell what vehicles they were, but noticed the manufacturers' emblems on their front bumpers. He stopped to make a left to drive towards the lot's exit.

Warren abruptly stopped to see vehicles passing by on the busy roads. He turned right and drove straight for the next ten miles. After two miles, there was a speed limit sign coming towards Warren's way. He pushed down on the throttle and climbed to sixty-five miles per hour. The road ahead of him is about to become a highway. The highway is suspended from the Hudson River. The sparkling in the river water was slowly dancing as his vehicle was moving. The wheels started to make that common whistling noise that drivers hear while they pass some bridges. The bridge lasted for about a mile.

The road becomes a freeway as it kept its straight pattern for the next four miles. It was surrounded by maple trees on both sides, which were ten feet from the road. The freeway had four lanes on both sides. The roads were newly paved, which made driving more smooth and comfortable. The lines dividing the lanes were their brightest shades of white. He activates his turning signal of his brake lights by gently pulling the switch down on the steering wheel. He was warning others surrounding him that he's going to make a right. His blinker started flashing between his brake lights. He slowed down to twenty-five miles per hour as he's about to drive up an entrance ramp.

As Warren drove up the ramp, there was a yellow thirty mile per hour limit, influencing him to accelerate. There were four ramps, giving two for each side that formed a cloverleaf shape on the roads. His body was swaying from the pull of the ramp until he had to merge into another freeway.

The freeway was nearly full of vehicles. Warren was on the last lane. While he was driving for half of a mile, he approached another speed limit as he accelerated to fifty-five miles per hour. The other three lanes were the fast lanes. There was a cement barrier to separate the two sides of the freeway.

As Warren kept driving for four more miles, he saw that there was a silver sedan driving next to him maintaining the exact speed. He noticed a black man inside the sedan. He was starting to feel uneasy as the man looked at him, dead in the eye. He peeked into the sedan and noticed that the man had black hair and was appearing to wear the same attire as he was. Warren slowed down in front of a yellow traffic light and waited for the drivers passing by. The light became red by the time he stopped. The man stopped with him as he was still staring down Warren with a serious and tempting look. Warren looked back at him, not knowing what to do as he was confused.

The light switched to green and Warren entered his street. The black man went the opposite of him. "What the hell was that all about?" Warren said to himself. Like the freeways, there were trees with their full and rich evergreen color on both sides. There was a speed limit on his road that made him decelerate to thirty-five miles per hour. He saw people's houses sparsely separated from each other on both sides with an alternating pattern.

Warren kept driving until he stopped after passing seven

two-story houses. He pulled into his driveway. His driveway's about the size of four car lengths. He stopped to park in front of his garage. He pulled the keys out of the transmission to hear the engine power down as the interior lights slowly faded. The sun was still shining as it reached the evening hours.

Warren exited his car with his equipment bag, stretched and walked to his front porch. His house was also two stories big. It was white on the outside with windows about ten feet from each other on the second floor. The house was pitch black as he walked in. He turned on the light switch to view a hallway and two flights of stairs. There was one flight of stairs on each side.

Warren walked to one side of the hallway to open a closet door. The closet was embedded into the wall. It was mostly composed of formal clothing, such as suit jackets with hangers, dress shirts and shoes. He shuffled his hand around the jackets in the top of the closet, eventually finding a hanger. He set his equipment bag down and took off his suit jacket to fit it around the hanger. He then placed his hungover jacket back in the closet. He took off his dress shoes and set them on the bottom.

Once Warren was done, he grabbed his equipment bag and walked into another room. He noticed a table with a set number of chairs. He stopped, and fumbled his arm around a light switch.

Warren turned on the light to view a kitchen. The kitchen was cream white around the walls and had two glass doors on the left side of the kitchen. While looking through the doors, he could see the plentiful grass and pleasant blue skies. The table was rectangular in shape and had eight chairs surrounding it. The table has a stained, wooden rim going around it as the chairs had the same texture.

Warren set his equipment bag on the tabletop and walked to the other side of the kitchen. There was another table, but twice as small and had the same texture. There were four chairs surrounding the smaller table. Around the table were two sets of kitchen countertops and cupboards that were metallic in texture. They were silver and had a

black stove that has touch sensitive screens on the top of it.

The stove was in between the cupboards, which were about

the same height as the stove, which was four feet. There was

also a sink with two doors on the bottom of it. There was a

window above the sink that viewed the vast farmlands of his

neighborhood.

While Warren was looking outside, he felt his phone

vibrate in his pocket accompanied by a ringtone. He looked at

the screen, but didn't recognize the number. He decided to

answer it anyway. "Hello?" he said.

"Hey, guess who this is." Warren immediately recognized

Phoenix's voice.

"Phoenix! Hey, how are you doing?" He sounded excited

to hear from her.

"I was about to ask you the same thing. What are you up

to right now?"

"Just got home. Thought I might relax around my house

for a little bit then head off to bed."

Warren walked out of his kitchen. He didn't go upstairs as he turned on a light in a room with a dryer and a washer. It was the laundry room. The room had Celeste blue walls with two laundry baskets by the machines all located on the right side. "It's all in a hard day's work when you get to meet someone," Warren said as he was pulling off his dress socks. Phoenix laughed joyfully. He pulled open the door of the washer and put the socks in there. He asks, "What's your favorite type of food?"

"Ehh...I have more of an appetite for Italian food than anything. How about you?"

"Same. I still have to look for places to eat, I have a day off tomorrow, so I'm good."

"Same here, I have a day off, too. Pick whatever restaurant you feel is a good one, after all, it was your idea. Like I said, surprise me." Warren blushed.

"I honestly can't wait for tomorrow. To be honest, I'm a little hungry right now," he said. Phoenix chuckled.

"Well, I guess I'll let you get off for the night."

"I can still talk for a few minutes, I'm just saying. Need to get myself situated here. Hold on a minute, I'm going to put you on speaker."

"Okay." Warren set his phone down in the shelf beside him as he continued to undress himself. He took off his dress shirt and loosened the belt around his dress pants and threw his shirt in the washer. He slid off his pants until he was wearing nothing but his underwear. He closed the washer and turned it on.

Warren walked to the shelf behind him and grabbed the Tide brand detergent and Downy fabric softener. He poured a cap full of each. He walked back to the washer and set the caps on top of it. He opened a flap on top of the washer and saw two pouches that stores the detergent and softener. He poured them in both pouches. After he was done, he walked to the sink on the other side to wash the caps off, and set them back to the shelf.

Warren grabbed his phone and walked up the staircase, "You still there, Phoenix?"

"Yeah, you're still available to talk, right?"

"Yeah, I'll talk for a few more minutes."

Warren admired the white, ceramic floors and walls of the hallway. He entered his bedroom. Most of it was white, including his walls, carpet, and bed. Some of the things that weren't white was the earlywood dresser and the entertainment system. The system was supported by metallic platforms that are welded together as it was about four and a half feet tall. The forty inch flat screen TV was suspended in the center of the wall just above the system. There was a digital cable box in the top compartment. He set the phone down by a lamp near his bed. He opened the bottom drawer of his dresser and found a pair of black pajamas.

Warren grabbed his phone. "So where do you live?" he asked while sitting on his bed, putting on his pajamas.

"I live right near the city, why do you ask?"

"So that I know where to pick you up for tomorrow."

"Okay."

"Well, I have to get off here, have to eat and get ready

for bed before too long."

"Okay, I guess I will talk to you later. Let me know if there's any changes."

"Okay, I'll see what I can come up with. I'll talk to you later."

"Looking forward to it, I'll see you tomorrow, bye."

"See you then." Warren put his phone back by the lamp. He walked back to his dresser and found a red T-shirt. He walked downstairs to the kitchen.

Warren walked towards the small table to see the refrigerator and the upright freezer. Not knowing what he's going to eat, he opened the freezer and looked through the items in there. There were numerous vegetable and meat products. He closed the freezer and walked to the refrigerator next to it. He found a bag of iceberg salad mix. Inside the bag was lettuce, carrots, radishes, and cabbage. He took the bag out and set it on the counter near the glass doors beside him. The glass doors projected the night skies from outside. He went back to the refrigerator to see various dairy products, sports drinks, and bottles of salad dressing. He looked at the dressing and grabbed a bottle of ranch.

Warren walked back to the counter and set the bottle of ranch near the salad mix. He crouched to open a cupboard door below the countertop. The door contained plastic bowls and containers. He grabbed a bowl as he took the mix and gently shook the contents out to fill it.

Warren gently squeezed the bottle of dressing and fixed his salad. He put the contents back in the refrigerator. He walked back to the salad bowl and pulled open a drawer below the countertop with silverware. He pulled out a spoon and stirred the mix. After he was done, he headed back upstairs.

As Warren entered his bedroom, he set the salad bowl on his dresser to get a tray. He crawled on the bed to grab the television remote to see that a local news channel was on.

The news channel was talking about updates with the economy. There were two tickers on the bottom of the screen that were scrolling to show the stock statistics of various companies. The channel showed a blue background with an equirectangular projection of the world. In front of the background were the news anchors behind a brown desk with a man and a woman sitting next to each other. They were both wearing business attire. Warren could see they were wearing navy blue suit jackets, white dress shirts, and navy blue ties. The man had black hair with a black mustache over the span of his lips. The woman had the same color of hair as the man. The man and woman start speaking, "The economy has been on the rise in the past couple of weeks."

"The economy that we know today may soon be gone as multi-million and billion dollar businesses have been gaining a massive growth. Small businesses becoming more known and are being able to catch up with their top-dollar competitors." Warren payed attention as he continued eating. There was a picture of dollar bills on the top right side of the screen. The television began to show people working at various types of workplaces, such as a man working in an office room with the same holographic interface Warren was using from the other day.

The male news anchor continued speaking as the montage of the workplaces was being shown, "Some of the businesses have been using and receiving what appears to be the works and concepts of advanced technologies. The man in the office room is using some kind of touch-sensitive computer screen with a holographic keyboard. The numerous designers of these computers said that these are made to eliminate the use of bulky computer monitors and may improve efficiency and productivity in the business field."

"Wow, sounds expensive," the female anchor said.

The screen switched to a video showing the parking lot of an automotive dealership on a sunny day. The male news anchor resumes, "Some automotive dealerships have recently been bringing expensive taste to their customers. The choices of vehicles that were once hard to get are now becoming more common. Vehicle manufacturers, such as Audi, Maserati, and Mercedes-Benz are showing accelerated growth from increased sales. As the numbers of sales of the world's vehicle companies keep growing, the features for the future production of vehicles will contain advanced technologies, such as the infotainment system and flexible driving options. The demand of these features are steadily increasing as the levels of technology we're currently using are continuing to evolve."

Warren just got done with his salad as he inserted one more spoonful in his mouth. He then turned off the television. He grabbed his bowl and walked out of his bedroom. He went back downstairs and went into the kitchen. As he approached the sink, he turned on the faucet to let water run over the bowl. There were touch-sensitive displays behind the sink. He tapped the temperature settings and set the water to a warmer temperature.

Warren crouched down to open the cupboard doors below the sink to find bottles of dishwashing liquid, and a stack of towels. He grabbed a bottle of dishwashing liquid and a couple towels to wash and dry the bowl. He squeezed a droplet onto the bowl and started rubbing around it with the towel. He turned off the faucet and reset the temperature settings to default. He patted the bowl as it reflected the lights from the kitchen's ceiling. He put the bowl back and grabbed the wet towels and walked out of the kitchen.

Warren put the towels in the laundry basket and walked back upstairs. While in his bedroom, he grabbed the tray and set it back to its original place. He then went into the bathroom. There is a sink on one side with a mirror above it, reflecting the upper half of his body. He bent forward to open the cupboard doors below the sink and grabbed a green toothbrush with yellow accents. He pulled open a drawer below the sink to grab a tube of toothpaste. He squeezed it until it touched all of the bristles on the toothbrush. He looked himself in the mirror as he brushed his teeth.

Warren continuously brushed his teeth until he turned the faucet to rinse his toothbrush. As the faucet was running, he moved his hands over the cold running water until they were half full. He rinsed his mouth from the water in his hands and swished it around. Afterwards, he washed his hands with a squirt of hand soap beside of the sink. He

opened the pantry to see several towels and washcloths. He

grabbed a towel to dry his hands off. He then hung it over the

support bar behind him that holds towels.

Warren walked back to his bedroom. He walked to his

bed and pulled the sheets out as they folded. He turned the

bedroom light off as the only light remaining was the dimly lit

lamp by the folded bed sheets. He crawled into the sheets

until they covered him from the neck down. He turned the

lamp off as the room turned to pitch black. He grabbed his

phone by the lamp and tapped the "Alarm" settings. He set

his alarm for seven o'clock in the morning. He then slowly

closed his eyes to help him drift off to sleep.

Chapter 4: Full Of Surprises

April 28, 2012

The curtains of Warren's bedroom showed the dim, blue skies as he was still asleep on a quiet Saturday morning. He immediately woke up as his alarm went off. The alarm was loud enough to where it can be heard from two rooms. He grabbed his phone and tapped "Dismiss Alarm" and set it back down. He sat up as half of his body was covered in the blanket. He smeared his hands down his face and chin to wake himself up. He faced the curtains and stood up to walk in the hallway. He walked to the opposite end of the hallway and opened the last door to the right.

As Warren opened the door, he saw a room from what appears to be a home styled version of a workplace. The computer setup is just like traditional computers used in an average home. The setup he has is nothing compared to B&N Financing. There was a Windows desktop monitor with a two and a half foot tall desk holding it. The desk has a compartment with a tower on the bottom right side of it. He walked on the soft, cyan carpet and sat down in the black office chair. The chair has four silver stainless steel legs supported by swivel wheels. There was a white keyboard with keys that have black characters. He reached down to the bottom of the tower to press the power button.

The icon for Microsoft Windows 7 appeared. The computer was approaching the loading screen as the Windows logo was slowly fluctuating its brightness. Warren patiently waited as he stretched his arms and legs. While stretching, he put both of his hands to the back of his head to relax himself. As the computer projected the login screen, he sat up straight to type his password. His computer successfully logged him in to show his wallpaper of a

snapshot from outer space. It shows a planet on the bottom

being lit from a sun surrounded by thousands of stars. He

moved his mouse and clicked on the taskbar to open Google

Chrome as the browser displayed its search engine.

Warren was thinking about the conversation he had with

Phoenix last night. He still had to look for a restaurant for

later in the day. He was thinking about the settings,

atmospheres, and themes of numerous restaurants that are

densely scattered across the city. He immediately came up

with an idea for filling a weekend getaway. He clicked on the

search bar and typed in "Italian restaurants in New York City"

and pressed Enter. He was scrolling down through the results

to find a promising destination.

Warren found a website of a restaurant that got a four

and a half star rating. He clicked on the link to find out about

the restaurant and the reviews of it. The prices ranged up to

fifty dollars or more per reservation. He clicked on "See

Menu" below, where it said "Price" on the top left side and

checked out what they serve. The menu items were

categorized in Lunch, Dinner, and Dessert. He clicked on the

dinner section. The menu shows a decent amount of items,

but with exotic choices. The choices presented weren't

familiar to him as the names of the dishes appeared to be in

Italian. He looked at the antipasti menu, which meant *before*

the meal in Italian.

As Warren had no idea what the dishes were, he opened

up a new tab to type in the name of the dish he was looking

for, which was "Truffled beef carne cruda with parmigiano-

reggiano and watercress buds". He broke down the types of

food mixed into the dish. Carne cruda, which is raw meat,

parmigiano-reggiano, a type of cheese, and watercress, a

type of plant. He was convinced because of the perfectly

blended mix the meal provided.

Warren stood up and walked downstairs to his closet. He

shuffled through his roster of suit jackets and other pieces of

attire. He was also looking for dress shirts and pants for later

on in the evening. He selected a white dress shirt along with a black suit jacket and dress pants. The last couple things he grabbed were his dress socks and shoes.

After Warren returned to his bedroom, he turned the light on and set his clothes on his bed. He went over to the wooden, brown wardrobe by the right side of the room. He opened the wardrobe to see an ironing table with its top slanted to the left in the wardrobe's interior. There was a newly bought iron supported by a shelf in the wardrobe. He grabbed the ironing table and carried it to the center of the room. He unfolded its steel legs and set it straight to ready himself for ironing. He took the outlet of the iron and plugged it in. He took his white dress shirt and ironed it to remove the creases and wrinkles. The thick steam came out from the iron as he set his shirt flat on his bed. Next, he grabbed his dress pants. His pants were made of wool, so he set the temperature of his iron on the highest setting for best results.

After Warren was done ironing his pants, he grabbed his suit jacket and held it up against the ceiling light. He noticed that there's hair and dust on the front of the jacket. He took his jacket and walked into the bathroom to turn on the light. He walked to the sink and opened a drawer to find various combs and brushes. He grabbed a brush to brush off unwanted hair on the front of his jacket. Once he was done, the jacket was restored to its rich and defined color. He returned back to the bedroom and set the jacket back on his bed.

As boredom and excitement kicked in, Warren took his phone and decided to call Phoenix. The time read as ten o'clock in the morning. He hesitated as he wasn't sure if she was sleeping. He abruptly changed his mind and placed his phone in his pocket and resumed to preparing himself for the evening. He went downstairs into the kitchen and turned on the built-in digital radio above the stove and tuned to a local rock station. He was listening to the radio for an hour.

Warren decided to try calling Phoenix again. He pulled out his phone and dialed her number. After three rings, she answered, "Hello?"

"Hey, Phoenix, how are you?"

"I'm doing good, how about yourself?"

"Pretty well, actually. Just getting myself situated for later on tonight." Warren hasn't discussed about what time he's picking her up. He was walking anxiously around the kitchen. He sat down at the table by the glass doors. "Hey, at around seven o'clock, I'll be picking you up, how does that sound to you?" he questioned.

"That's fine by me. That gives me plenty of time to get ready."

"So, what are you up to right now?"

"Nothing really, just pouring myself a pot of coffee."

"What kind of coffee is it?"

"Vanilla, it's a creamer, it gives it a little sweetener when you mix it, you know?"

"Yeah, I really don't like my coffee plain either." Phoenix chuckled. Warren got up from the table and walked towards the glass doors. He noticed the grass glaring from the sunlight as there was no sign of clouds. "It's a beautiful day outside," he said.

"I know, right? It's been nice out for the past couple of weeks."

"Yeah." Warren hesitated, but realized he had to get ready for the outing. He almost forgot to ask where she lives, "Where do you live, exactly?"

"Well, I live just on the very end of the suburbs of New York City. It's on the right side of the road."

"Hold on, let me get a piece of paper to write that down." Warren walks out of the kitchen and went upstairs to enter his office room.

Warren went to the computer station to open a drawer full of fresh notebooks and unopened packs of loose leaf paper. He rips open the top of the laminated packaging of loose leaf paper and sets it near his monitor. He gently slides a piece of paper out of the packaging to write down the address of Phoenix's house as she gives him it. "Okay, thank you. I'm going to have to let you go for right now. I have to finish getting ready. I'll let you know when I'm on my way there," he said.

"Okay, I'll let you know when I'm all ready."

"Okay, I'll talk to you later and I'll see you then, bye."

"Bye." Warren smiled as he ended the call. He went back downstairs into the kitchen.

Time passed as Warren was sitting by the glass doors. He looked at his phone to see that the time read as four o' clock in the evening. He stood up from the table and walked upstairs. He went into his bedroom to grab his clothes and into the bathroom. He'll be leaving his suit jacket on his bed until he is ready to leave.

Warren turned the light on and closed the bathroom door. He hung his clothes over on the support bar on the right side. He opened up the pantry door and grabbed two blue towels and a washcloth to prepare himself for taking a shower. He crouched down to the bottom of the pantry and grabbed a bar of soap. He opened the shower cabinet door to turn on the warm water. Upon closing the door, he started taking a shower. The thick steam from inside the cabinet escaped to the ceiling as he was washing his body.

After ten minutes, Warren took the towel to dry himself off and started getting dressed. He put on his dress shirt and buttoned it up to his neck. He then put on a pair of underwear along with his pants and creased his shirt under it. Once he was done, he zipped his pants up. He puts on his dress socks and tied his shoes before he started brushing his teeth.

After a couple minutes, Warren set the toothbrush down and filled his hands half full of water. He inserted the water into his mouth and swished it around. He spit out the water and washed his hands with the yellow bar of soap next to the sink. He grabbed a towel from the pantry to dry his hands off.

Warren started looking for a bottle of cologne. He stored it at the bottom of the pantry. The shelf comprised brands that were luxurious in origin. He picked up a glass bottle that was in the shape of a flask. He walked back to the mirror and sprayed a couple whiffs on his chestal region and armpits.

Warren also found a bottle of mousse next to the cologne. He grabbed the mousse and looked in the mirror. He squirted a quarter-sized amount on the palm of his hand. He began to smear it on his hands. He placed his hands on his hair and mixed it around. He pulled open a drawer below the sink to find a comb to stick his hair up. Once he was done combing, all of it was creased upward and styled like a buzz cut. After he got done getting dressed, he went back to his bedroom.

Warren walked to his dresser and pulled open the middle drawer to find a black leather belt. He closed the drawer and looped the belt around his pants. He grabbed his suit jacket and put it on. He is now ready to go after he buttoned his jacket and turned off the light as he walked out.

Warren took his phone out to see that the time was five-thirty in the evening. He turned the bathroom light off as he was walking downstairs. As he walked into the kitchen to turn the light off, he started to dial Phoenix's number. "Hello?" she answered.

"Hey, I'm about to leave my house, you all ready to go?"

"Yeah, I just need to fix my hair and I'm all set for

tonight."

"Okay, I have to go, I gotta start my car and I'll be on my

way."

"Okay, I'll see you then."

"Looking forward to it,' Warren calmly laughed in joy. "I'll

see you in a little bit."

"Bye." Warren dismissed the call and placed his phone in

his pocket. He went back upstairs and straight to his dresser.

He picked up his dark, brown Italian leather wallet to check

how much he has in bills. He closed his wallet and placed it in

his pocket and went back downstairs. He walked into the

kitchen and back in the hallway to turn off the remaining

lights throughout the house.

He walked to the front entrance door and saw the clear,

blue, evening skies outside as he opened the door. He walked

down the steps of his porch and walked to his Mercedes-

Benz. He opened the door and climbed into the seat. He

inserted his key in the ignition and started the vehicle. He

took a few moments to set up the navigation system. He

typed in Phoenix's address on the screen from the paper he wrote on earlier in the morning and buckled his seat belt.

Warren set the vehicle in reverse. He slowly tapped the throttle until he reached the end of his driveway to look for oncoming vehicles. There was a red coupe passing by as he was waiting to enter the road. He turned to the left to enter the opposite lane from where the coupe drove. He put the vehicle into drive and accelerated to thirty-five miles per hour. After driving past the seven houses, he stopped to wait for other drivers.

Warren turned right and entered the freeway. The navigation system told him to keep going straight for the next seven miles. The trees on both sides were swaying slowly as the vehicle was moving. A speed limit sign was approaching his way as he accelerated to fifty-five miles per hour. The evening sun was delivering its orange and yellow hues in the center of the sky.

About three miles into the freeway, Warren approached a bridge. He heard the humming noise as his vehicle was rolling across the bridge. The bridge lasted for about a mile. The freeway wasn't as packed from when he was arriving home from work. The roads were open as it was moderately dense.

After driving for three more miles, Warren approached a road going downwards. He activated his turn signal as his taillight started blinking, warning other drivers around him. He turned right on the descending road and merged into a highway. The highway lasted for about three miles. The highway has a white barrier to separate the two sets of four lanes. The navigation system said to turn right onto a street for the last road of his destination.

Warren stopped to turn on Phoenix's street. The speed limit on her street forced him to decelerate to twenty-five miles per hour. He remembers her telling him that her house is located to the right from where he's driving as he is carefully looking at the houses. The sunset was getting lower as he looked across the rich, grassy plains in the neighborhood.

Warren stopped in the driveway of a white two-story house and set the transmission in park. The house had two A-framed sections on the second floor. The A-frames had two squared windows with curtains' shadows behind them. He was quite nervous as he exited the vehicle and walked on the driveway. The driveway showed an orange sedan with a Pontiac emblem parked in front of a garage door as he was walking towards the porch steps of the front yard. He looked at the rear of the sedan to see that it was a Pontiac G8.

Warren walked up the steps to get a close up of the modern setting of the porch. The porch was rather larger than his. It was about one and a half to two times the size from his estimate. The mood of the porch was the origin of relaxation. There were two chairs on the right side. The chairs were wooden as they were painted white and were on all fours. The bench from the left side of him was also white as well. About a few inches of the back of the bench can be seen from the window behind it. The window projected a vibrant, sequoia color with curtains curved behind it.

Warren walked towards the front door. The door was made of artistic glass as it had curves that were slightly risen on all sides. He had to be extra careful when knocking. He gently knocked on the door five times, waiting for the person to open the door. He took a deep breath to reduce the stress from his body.

A person opened a door behind the glass door. Warren couldn't tell who it was. He saw a person wearing a sparkling emerald green dress. He was anxious to see who it was, but kept his composure. As the person opened the door, he noticed it was Phoenix. Her curly blonde hair was reflectively shining from the brilliant white interior of her home. She was carrying a dark brown leather purse that extended down to her hip with the strap on her shoulder. She was elated to see him as she smiled. "Warren!" she said excitedly. She ran up to him and gave him a hug as he did the same.

"Phoenix, hey! How are you?"

"I'm really happy right now, happy that you came here!" Warren felt relieved when he saw her. They felt relaxed as they were still hugging. "It's good to see you again," Phoenix said calmly.

"You, too, you look really nice."

"Why, thank you! I appreciate that, Warren." They let go of each other and stand face to face.

"You ready to go?" Warren said.

"Ready when you are, Warren."

"Okay, sounds like a good answer to me." They laughed with each other as they walked down the porch steps.

"Nice car!" Phoenix said.

"Thank you, saved up a lot of money for this thing. It has the best features that money can buy for a vehicle. Touchscreen infotainment system, fancy interior, comfortable seats, the list goes on, Phoenix." She wasn't familiar with the word, "infotainment."

"I'm sorry, but what's infotainment?" she said, laughing in confusion.

"I'll tell you when we get in the car." Warren opened the door to the driver's seat while Phoenix was standing beside him. She walked around the front bumper until she was standing by the passenger door. She waited until Warren unlocked the doors.

"Nice, interior, too!" Phoenix said as they were climbing in the vehicle.

"Oh, you haven't seen anything yet." Phoenix raised her eyebrow and kept her smile. "What do you mean by that?" she replied.

"You'll see." Warren started the vehicle.

"Wow!" Phoenix said as she saw the interior light up. She was even more surprised by the roar of the engine. She saw the touchscreen infotainment system in the middle of the dashboard. "That is so cool, Warren! I'm impressed!"

"That's what a luxury car brand can do for you." Warren puts the vehicle in reverse. He gently let his foot on the throttle until he stopped at the end of her driveway. There was no sign of vehicles. He turned left until he was straight on the road. He set it into drive and drove straight. He stopped at the end of the road to wait for oncoming vehicles. After waiting for ten seconds, he turned right and drove straight on the highway for the next ten miles. He's about to explain to Phoenix about the infotainment system, "So, basically, an infotainment system is a feature of electronics that uses information and mixes itself around with entertainment. Take the news for example, you're listening to a news station while driving. You're gathering information as you're driving on the road without distraction. As for the entertainment, you're listening to music as you drive, so, yeah, but it doesn't only have the news and music aspects. Those are just a couple of the many features of what an infotainment system has to offer. It's a pretty neat feature."

"Oh, that's cool, do you mind if I play around with it for a minute?"

"No, I don't care, but yeah, can't play with it for too long because I have the navigation system activated. It's hard to find out which road to go on without looking at the directions, you know?"

"Yeah, I know what you mean." Phoenix was amazed by

the way the navigation system was projecting its heads-up display. The street name was at the top center of the screen as the speed was on the bottom left. The distance to the next road was located on the bottom right as the compass was located to the center right. The bottom center was accompanied by a red arrow, indicating the driver's position on the road. As Phoenix was about to tap the menu button on the left side of the screen, a female voice said to merge right onto the freeway in the next four hundred yards. She was startled by the loud volume of the voice. "Wow, that's loud!" she said.

"And it's fast, too. Best GPS I've ever used. Definitely beats the leading brand."

"I could tell because of how smooth the screen moves as you go."

"Here, I'll put some music on if that's what you were looking for," Warren said.

There were buttons on the right side of the steering wheel. They're used for the infotainment system. The button

Warren was going to select was towards the edge of the steering wheel. He pressed the MENU button as the navigation screen collapsed and shrank into the center. The main menu zoomed in on the screen, giving him a variety of settings and features. He pressed the up arrow on the MENU button three times until the menu was highlighting "Music/Audio".

Warren pressed the ACTION button to enter the wide range of thousands of songs. The music was categorized and organized into folders, such as "Artists" and "Genres". He presses the button on the "Genres" section. The screen swipes over to the left of the previous screen. He scrolls down through the wide range of genres while holding the down arrow on the MENU button. "So what kind of music do you like? I have rock, country, electronica, you name it," he said.

"I like any kind of music to be honest with you," Phoenix said.

"What's one of your favorite bands at least?"

"Umm....I really don't know. I have a lot of them."

"Same here, if there's a certain song or band you want to listen to, let me know, and I'll see if I have it."

"Okay." Warren pressed the RETURN button next to the ACTION button to go back to the "Music/Audio" menu. He pressed the down arrow on the MENU button to highlight the "Artists" folder. He pressed the ACTION button to view the hundreds of potential artists in the twenty-seven folders of the menu. The folders were organized in alphabetical order with the acception of a folder for numbers. As the menu swiped over, there was a "Shuffle" option on top of the "A" folder. He pressed the ACTION button.

The music started playing a popular song from the band, Nickelback. The music made the atmosphere in the vehicle more vibrant for Warren and Phoenix. "This is a good song," Phoenix said, smiling. The song that was playing is one of her favorite songs from the band. They bobbed their heads back and forth to the music. The arrangement of the music was composed of moderately complex melodies from the heavy guitars and intense drums throughout the song. As Warren approached another road, he activated his turn signal on the right side of his vehicle. He ascended on a road and hung his vehicle to the right as he was turning in a full circle on an entrance ramp.

Once Warren got off the ramp, the navigation system told him to keep going straight for the next five miles. He quickly glanced to his right to see the skyline of New York City. Most of the buildings he saw were tall as they were piercing the clear, sunset skies. The sun still projected its faded orange, yellow hues as it formed a semicircle, covering the skyline. "Beautiful," he said in awe. Phoenix looked in the same direction as him.

"I know, New York City is a beautiful place." Phoenix replied. They smiled at each other in a joyous manner. Warren noticed a speed limit sign and accelerated to sixty-five miles per hour.

After Warren drove for five miles, he activated his turn signal as his right amber taillight was blinking. He descended down an exit ramp and decelerated to thirty miles per hour.

As the vehicle touched ground, the navigation system told Warren to keep going straight for the next two miles. The road he was driving through had small buildings on both sides, involving small businesses. He noticed another speed limit and accelerated to thirty-five miles per hour.

As Warren drove for a mile on the road, the city's tall buildings were nearly doubling in height as he was driving closer. He approached a stop sign and caught a glimpse of the exterior of the city's infrastructure. He was waiting for passing vehicles to provide a clear space for him to enter the road. He turned right to enter the outer perimeters of the city as some of the buildings were lit up. The evening skies became dimmer. The lights on some of the buildings featured numerous advertisements. The advertisements featured various products, businesses including Warren's workplace, upcoming films, and so on. Some have mirrored walls with the combined light of the sky. The sun was reflecting off of the clean texture of the buildings' walls. The vehicles driving past him including himself had their headlights on to light up the roads.

While Warren was looking around the city, the navigation system told him to make a left to head southwest into Chambers Street. He turned as there was a clear gap for him. The road he turned on had buildings on both sides. The tallest building in his perspective was the main headquarters of a finance company, but wasn't his workplace. The navigation system told him to drive straight for the next two hundred yards. He slowly put his foot on the brake as the navigation system told him he's close to his destination.

As Warren came to a complete stop, he parked in between two vehicles by a restaurant on the left side of the road. The road was already packed with vehicles by the time he arrived. The name of the restaurant was Del Posto, which is an Italian-themed restaurant. The sign above the entrance was rectangular and black in color. The word, DEL was located on the left side of the sign. The word, POSTO was about twice the size of DEL and is located off to the right. Once he parked the vehicle, Phoenix looked at him and smiled gleefully. "I like the name," she said.

"Told me to surprise you, said you liked Italian." Phoenix blushed as her cheeks started to redden. He looked at her, "You ready?"

"Yeah, I am." Warren and Phoenix unbuckled their seat belts and exited the vehicle. He was standing on the light, gray sidewalk below the restaurant sign. He patiently waited for her as she was walking towards him.

Warren and Phoenix are standing beside each other as they walked to the glass doors of the entrance. As they walked in front of the doors, he opened the door for her. She looked at him in surprise. "Why, thank you," Phoenix said to him while smiling. Warren nodded his head, "You're welcome."

Warren and Phoenix walked into the lobby of the restaurant. There was a tan stretch of floor in the center with a pattern of tan and navy blue trapezoids. They noticed that the room is arranged in a layout of luxury, relaxation, and romance. The ceiling was black as it reflected the sunlight from the glass doors. As they looked straight, there was a table with two clear vases of flowers located about ten feet away from where they're standing. About ten feet from the table was a black wooden stool. The stool has a white bowl of fruit as there was a small, black fence forming a ring behind it. Behind the ring was a white flight of stairs in between a guardrail on each side. In between the small, ringed fence was two curved barriers with lamps sitting on top of them. The white lampshades were supported by the luxurious sight of their golden legs. The curved barriers are white on their tops as the walls of the barriers were painted in dark brown. To Warren's right, he saw three square tables with white tablecloths covering over them. The tables were occupied as the people sitting at them were wearing informal attire.

Phoenix looked to her left to see that people were sitting at tables that were accompanied by brown, leather benches, but couldn't see them fully. "I can help whoever's waiting." Warren heard a man in the background, but couldn't tell if the man was talking to him. They were standing a few feet away from the voice they heard. He looked around to see where it was coming from. He looked to his right to see a man looking at him and Phoenix.

The man was standing behind a counter as he was organizing reservations and seating orders. The counter was set up with a Windows computer along with a cash register beside it. The man has black hair with tanned skin and was wearing a black, long sleeved dress shirt with a vest over top of it. The vest was that of a greenish yellow color with patterns of diamonds and thick, red outlines. There were gray outlines inside the red ones. The outlines continued to shrink down until there were solid black diamonds in between the outlines.

Warren and Phoenix walked to the counter to greet the man behind it. The man smiled while showing his pearly, white teeth. "Hi," they said to the man.

"Good evening, how are you today?"

"Doing good," Warren said.

"Good," Phoenix said.

"What can I help you with today?" the man said politely.

"Umm...I'm here to make a reservation for two, please?" Warren said.

"Alright, I'll get you both situated in just one moment." The man was typing on the computer to search for all available tables on the first floor. "What is your name, sir?" the man continued.

"Warren Leyton, L-E-Y-T-O-N." The man opened the receipt window on the computer screen and typed his name. The man is now talking to Phoenix, "And what is your name, ma'am?"

"Phoenix Hadaway, H-A-D-A-W-A-Y."

As the man completed the reservation order, the small display on the back of the cash register showed the price as the receipt paper was being printed out from the top. "Okay, that's going to be a total of sixty-two dollars and ninety-seven cents," the man said.

"Okay," Warren said. He puts his hand in his pocket to pull out his wallet to skimmer through numerous dollar bills.

He continued looking until he pulled out a fresh fifty dollar bill and twenty dollar bill. Warren gave the man the money. The man pushed a red button on the top of the cash register. The button opened the tray of bills and coins arranged from the lowest value to the highest. Warren looked to see that each of the bills' sections were halfway full as well as the coins. The restaurant didn't accept half-dollar and dollar value coins. The man pulled out a five-dollar bill and two one-dollar bills with three pennies to give him his change, "Here's your change, sir." The man set the bills and coins in Warren's hand.

"Thank you, sir," Warren said. He placed his wallet and loose change back in his pocket.

The man walked out of the counter to show Warren and Phoenix to their table, "Your table will be on your left from where the hanging ceiling lights and the chandeliers are. Follow me, I'll show you where your table is."

"Alright," Warren said.

"Okay," Phoenix said.

Warren and Phoenix walk with the man. The man was walking faster than them as it was hard to keep up. As they entered the room, the man stopped to show them their table. He let both of his arms and hands out as he presented Warren and Phoenix's table. Most of the tables were taken from other customers while some were waiting for their meals. The tabletop was a mix of the colors, beige and tan. The table was sitting by a wall with thin, wooden, decorative fencing across it. The wall was wide enough to where eight tables can fit beside it. Warren and Phoenix walked to the man. "Here's your table. If you guys need anything and if you have any questions, feel free to come to the lobby counter and I'll try to help you guys out the best I can. I have to get back to the counter, the line's starting to get bigger. Enjoy your evening!" the man said.

"Thank you!" said Warren.

"Uh-huh."

Warren and Phoenix take a seat at their table. The seats were rather comfortable. They were the color of dark sienna, which is a dark shade of brown, and were made of leather.

They sat across from each other. Phoenix took the strap of

her purse off of her shoulder and set it next to her. They

looked at each other while smiling and start a conversation.

"Wow, Warren, this is a nice place, and big, too!" Phoenix said

quietly as she looked around in awe. Warren laughed.

"It's beautiful here," Warren said.

"I'm glad you picked this place!"

"Same here."

Phoenix smiled, causing Warren to blush and chuckle.

The lights from the ceiling reflected down on her ocean, blue

eyes. Her blonde hair was also reflected upon as it increased

the vibrant quality of her hair. Warren was flattered and was

already enjoying his evening.

While Warren and Phoenix were admiring each other, a

couple chefs were walking from the lobby. They were coming

towards their way. They were moving steel carts that carried

trays and plates with food and drinks that were served in

glassware. The drinks were on the bottom compartments as

the trays and plates were on top.

Warren and Phoenix didn't notice that a waiter was approaching their way to collect their orders. The waiter was wearing a white dress shirt with a black vest, dress pants and shoes. Warren noticed he was carrying a clipboard full of paper with a pen. The waiter kept walking until he was standing at their table. "How are you guys doing this evening?" said the waiter. He has an Italian accent. The waiter was very young as he's in his early twenties. He has black hair with white skin.

"Good," said Warren and Phoenix.

"I am going to be your waiter for the evening, taking your orders. If the lobbyist hasn't discussed this with you already, if you have any general questions about anything within Del Posto, feel free to call me back down here, go up to the lobby, or talk to a staff member and we'll help you the best we can. We're more than welcome to help anybody."

"Thank you, sir," said Warren.

"You're very welcome, any kind of beverages you guys

want? We have a wide variety of drinks to choose from. We have water, soft drinks, coffee drinks, and alcohol. I'm going to start with you, sir. What beverage would you like for the evening?"

"Umm.....I really don't know," Warren said in confusion. He laughed as the man described the choices of drinks as Phoenix laughed with Warren. "Do you have a menu for drinks as well?" he continued.

"Ah, yes, I have the menus for both our dishes and beverages. Would you guys like for me to come back later?"

"Sure, we would like that. This is our first time here actually," Phoenix said.

"Oh, yeah? Do you like it here?"

"Yeah, the atmosphere of this place is overwhelming, it's really beautiful here."

"Thank you." The waiter smiled and gave them their menus. They weren't thick at all, but the items were selective in variety as well as the beverages.

"I'm going to give you guys these menus to take a look at

our items. If you need more time to decide on what you want, we're more than happy to allow that. So guys, take your time, relax a little bit while you're at it. Make the most out of your evening," the waiter insisted. He walked back the way he came from. "Thank you!" said Phoenix as she raised her voice, but didn't yell or scream.

"You're welcome!"

Phoenix and Warren had a shocked look on their faces.

"Wow, the people here are really nice!" Phoenix said quietly.

"Yeah, I'm starting to like the service here already," Warren said. They laughed with each other. Phoenix sighed to calm herself down. "Okay, let's see what they have here," he said to himself.

Warren and Phoenix opened up their drink menus. The food and drinks are categorized in the Italian language, but the items were in English. They scanned through the menu with the swift movements from their eyes. They smoothly scrolled down with their fingers. While Warren was looking, the item list revealed a wide range of drinks to choose from.

In the cocktails section, there were different kinds of wines

and rums from different countries as well as scotches and

whiskeys. He was curious about all of them. He found them

rather interesting as they had their own unique ingredients

assigned to them. He looked back to the first page to find the

water and soft drinks. He found that they make their own

sparkling water. He decides on the sparkling water as well as

Phoenix.

Warren and Phoenix opened the food menus to reveal

the dishes. The restaurant was serving dinner due to the

dimly lit sun from outside.

Warren found the dish he checked out from his house.

He looked at Phoenix to see her still scrolling down the menu.

She wasn't sure what she wanted yet. "These menu items, I

have never heard of these before," Phoenix said.

"Me, neither," Warren said. Without moving her head,

Phoenix saw the same waiter that greeted them walking to

their way. He had the same clipboard and pen.

"You guys ready to take your orders?" the waiter said.

"What drinks and dishes can I get you for the evening? I'm going to start off with you, sir." The waiter was looking at Warren. He clicked his black retractable ballpoint pen open to take orders. Once the waiter looked at him, Warren looked down the menu to locate the dish he found earlier.

"Umm....I'll take some sparkling water, please," Warren said.

"Okay, small, medium, or large?"

"Umm...A medium, please?"

"And what dish would you like for the evening?"

"Well, I'll have the truffled beef carne cruda with parmigiano-reggiano and watercress buds." The waiter quickly wrote down his order as he looked down at Phoenix. She looked down to relocate her choices.

"Umm....I'll take some sparkling water as well, please," she said.

"Small, medium, or large?"

"Medium."

"And what dish would you like for the evening?"

"I'll take the spaghetti with dungeness crab, sliced jalapeño, and minced scallion, please." The waiter took her order.

"Is that it?" said the waiter. Warren and Phoenix looked at each other. Warren looked up at the waiter.

"I believe that will be it, sir," he said.

"Okay, it'll probably take about five minutes for the drinks, and your dishes will probably take about twenty minutes for preparation."

"Okay." The waiter walked away. Warren and Phoenix saw that the waiter was walking into a brightly lit room, assuming it's the kitchen.

"You know something, Phoenix?" Warren said.

"What's that, Warren?"

"Part of my heritage is also Italian."

"Really? Same here, I have a big interest in Italian culture."

"Same here."

"You know, I'm glad I picked this place."

"Same here, it's beautiful in here, Warren." They smiled. They felt different about each other at this point as they started to blush. They felt closer as if they have known each other for a while.

"You're really beautiful," Warren said. Phoenix laughed and was blushing even more. "You know, I'm glad I got a chance to meet you."

"Good thing we have the same lunch together," Phoenix winked at him. Warren said, "I thought of this while I was looking for a restaurant. After we're done here, I'm going to take you someplace special."

"Well, you're just full of surprises, aren't you?"

"That's why I make my living at a financing corporation. Besides, I felt like making an appointment for a weekend getaway anyways."

"Good thing I have the weekend off." They kept their smiles and set their arms on the table. They grabbed each other's hands and locked them together as they locked eyes.

Warren and Phoenix didn't notice the waiter until they see a silver, rolling steel cart in front of him. The cart carried dishes of food and beverages with their dishes on top as the bottom held the beverages. The waiter grabbed the two plates containing Phoenix's spaghetti and Warren's beef. He then set them on the table. The waiter crouched down again to grab their glasses of sparkling water. He set them down next to their dishes when he stood back up. "Thank you very much, sir," Phoenix said politely.

"You're very welcome, since this is your first time here, I'm going to briefly tell you about how you pay." The waiter's now talking to both of them, "Del Posto allows customers to pay after their meals because the service and atmosphere of this restaurant is meant to represent fine living and luxury. We allow our customers to enjoy their meals without having to pay before receiving them, well, just as long as you have enough money." The waiter laughed. "So like I said before, if you guys have any questions about the food or the drinks, the paying system we have here, or any other general questions, you can let me or any of the other staff members know, okay?"

"Alright," said Warren and Phoenix. This time, the waiter is going straight with a couple dishes and a compartment full of beverages in the cart to serve other customers. The waiter didn't get far as Warren was about to say something. "Thanks again," he raised his voice, but without yelling.

"You're welcome." The waiter continued walking while pushing the cart. He turned right to deliver other customers' meals. Warren and Phoenix looked down at their dishes and unwrapped the napkins containing their utensils.

Warren and Phoenix picked up their forks and started eating. On Phoenix's spaghetti, it was made of yellow egg noodle with small pieces of jalapeño peppers and scallions mixed around it. On Warren's beef, it was in pieces as it mixed with the cheese and the watercress. Phoenix inserted the fork in the spaghetti and spun it around until its end was halfway full.

Phoenix raised her eyebrow as she tasted the spaghetti.

After she swallowed, she widened her eyes and curled her lips, indicating that she liked it. "This is really good," she said.

Warren took his knife and fork and started cutting the beef with a few watercress buds on it. His eyes were shifting and his cheek was bulging out as he was testing the beef, indicating he liked it. "Mmm," he said. Phoenix looked at him, "How's the beef?"

"Delicious, how's your spaghetti?"

"I love it. It's well cooked."

"Definitely worth the money for the first time," Warren said before he sipped his sparkling water.

After fifteen minutes, Phoenix saw the waiter. He noticed they were halfway done with their dishes. The waiter made a gesture by holding both of his hands together. "Hey, guys, I'm just checking on how you are doing back here. Is the food alright?" the waiter said.

"Yeah," said Warren and Phoenix.

"Any refills on your sparkling water?"

"We're good," said Warren.

"Okay, I'm going to take off now and let you guys finish your meals, have to get other customers' orders in."

"Okay, sir," Warren said. The waiter walked as they continued eating. After ten minutes, they were done along with their sparkling water and wiped their mouths with the napkins. "Probably not going to be hungry later," Warren said.

"Same here, that was some good food."

"Do you get out a lot?" Warren asked Phoenix, but she was shy to talk.

"No, not really, never really had the time. Just got a job at where you're working at. Plus I met you and all of that. This weekend's been crazy for me. Busy one, too."

"Yeah, it sometimes gets hectic at B&N." Phoenix chuckled, but shifted her eyes down to the table. Warren was thinking something was wrong, "Phoenix." She looked up. "You alright?"

"Oh, yeah, I'm fine."

"Alright, I was thinking there was something wrong."

"Oh, no, I'm fine, but thank you though. That was nice of

you." Phoenix smiled at Warren. He smiled back.

The waiter came back. He didn't have the clipboard with him as he only has a small red piece of paper in his hand. He set the paper down on the table. "Here's the bill to your dishes for the evening. Enjoy the rest of your night," the waiter said.

"Thank you, sir," said Warren politely. The bill totaled up to a little over sixty dollars, the estimate of their reservations.

Warren pulled out his wallet and grabbed a fifty-dollar bill, a ten-dollar bill, and two one-dollar bills and set them on the table. To let the staff know that they received excellent service, he set out a ten-dollar bill as a tip. He closed his wallet and put it back in his pocket. He grabbed his phone to check the time to see it was seven minutes to eight o'clock. He put the phone back and smiled at Phoenix. "Ready to go?" he said.

"Yeah, just need to get my purse and I'm ready."

"Take your time, I'll wait, no rush."

Phoenix grabbed the strap of her purse and walks beside

Warren as he stands up. They turned their heads and smiled joyfully.

Warren and Phoenix walked until they were a few feet from the reservation counter. The man that organized their reservations was still working behind it. As they opened the glass doors and walked outside, there was barely any light in the sky as the streets were lit up. The lamps were lit all around them. Each of them have a distance of a few feet apart.

Warren and Phoenix walk to his sedan. He reached in his pocket and pulled out his car keys. In the middle of the door panel was the shape of a curved upside-down trapezoid. There was an L-shaped door latch. He pressed a button with a picture of an unlocked combination lock to open the doors.

Warren and Phoenix climbed into the vehicle and buckled their seat belts. They closed the doors as he started the car. The speakers immediately kicked in as it directly left off with the song they were listening to as it was almost over.

Once the song was over, the music played a popular song

from Green Day. The beginning had tremolo guitars playing in the background. He kept pressing the down arrow of the MENU button until the screen highlighted "Navigation" and pressed the ACTION button.

Warren tapped the arrow on the screen to show a text box with the word, "Destination" above it and typed in a different address. Phoenix looked down as he was typing it in. She was confused as she raised her eyebrow. Once he typed in the address, she looked back up at him. "You're up to something," she said. He looked at her flirtatiously.

"You'll see." Warren drove for about two hundred feet until he stopped in front of a four-way intersection. He looked up at the traffic lights ahead of him as he waits for the oncoming vehicles to pass.

After the light turned green, Warren turned right and accelerated to twenty-five miles per hour. The road he was surrounded by had several buildings with multiple stories. The buildings were no more than ten stories along with several small businesses. The small businesses were no more than two stories. By the sidewalks, there are long columns of

vehicles parked off to the sides. As he continued driving, the

scale of the buildings got bigger as he seen some parking lots.

"New York City is such a big city. It's bigger than what some

people think," Phoenix said.

"They even have their own park in the center of the city.

It's crazy of how much stuff you can do in a place like this,"

Warren said.

"That's why they call it The City That Never Sleeps."

As Warren made a right onto 9th Avenue, the roads

doubled in size as they were school crossing zones. A

moderate amount of pedestrians were walking on both sides.

There are two white lines on the road that got bigger with

white arrows in the center as the double lane roads are

separated by a crosswalk. He noticed trees evenly spaced

from each other. As he drove further, he noticed various

bushes in vases.

Warren turned left to enter West 14th Street. The

buildings got bigger in scale as he stopped in front of a traffic light. After the light turned green, he drove straight for the next mile. More of the potentially thousands of small businesses kept showing up as he drove. He eventually made a right onto 2nd Avenue. 2nd Avenue was packed with vehicles as they hung off both sides. He turned left on another street, confusing Phoenix from where he's taking her.

Warren stopped as he saw a building that had a sign with constantly flashing neon lights with different colors. He peeked to see there were also glass doors like the entrance at Del Posto.

Warren parked his vehicle near the sidewalk. "We're here," he said. He got out of the vehicle. He walked to the passenger door and opened it for Phoenix. He held his arm out, "Follow me." She hesitated. Phoenix was convinced and grabbed Warren's hand. She was being extra cautious not to trip on her sparkling, gold high heels.

Warren and Phoenix walked towards the glass doors as they're holding hands. He opened the door to enter the building. They looked around the interior to notice the style of a formal dance venue. It was dimly lit, but set a romantic

atmosphere. "What do you think?" he said.

"Warren, you read my mind." The floor was waxed as it

shined from the ceiling lights. The reflections of the disco ball

from the ceiling were slowly spinning on the floor. There's a

large amount of couples dancing, as the room was spacious.

Warren and Phoenix saw a man behind a white counter.

The counter has a black, slim desktop computer with a silver

metal bin. Warren didn't tell her he bought tickets in

advance. The man has black hair with skin that looked like he

was a fan of the sun. The man wore a black suit jacket with a

white dress shirt and a red tie creased nicely in the middle.

"You have tickets?" the man said to Warren.

"Yes, I sure do," Warren said. He took his wallet out to

look for his tickets. He reached in the bill compartment to pull

out two yellow tickets and inserted them through the small

opening of the bin.

"Okay, thank you very much, sir. Enjoy your evening!" the

man said.

"Thanks, you too!" Warren said.

Warren and Phoenix walked to the center of the dance floor and smiled. They were thinking of how to start the dance as the music of choice was either electronica, dubstep, or hard dance music. The song started off with intense percussive techno hits on a cinematic scale. The tonal quality was mostly made of noise and glitches.

Warren and Phoenix started dancing rhythmically to the music. Behind them was a disk jockey with a white dress shirt. He was standing in front of a set of turntables. The turntables were black as its rims were chrome with a silver tone. Beside the turntables was a silver Lenovo brand laptop with a black keyboard. Above the disk jockey were light projectors implanted into the wall as they spun around simultaneously. They lit up the entire room to increase the mood and enthusiasm of the music.

Warren and Phoenix began solo dancing, but were still together as they were a couple feet from each other. He was head banging and moved his arms rhythmically and shifted his back. Phoenix was dancing differently than him. She was shifting her body up and down while moving in a zigzag pattern. She was also moving her arms rhythmically in front of her face.

Warren and Phoenix decided to get closer together as they stood their bodies straight and smiled. He let his hand out as Phoenix grabbed it. He grabbed her arm and put it to his shoulder. They began moving as they took big steps by turning in ninety degree angles. They were dancing the same way until they heard a full four bar measure of the song. Warren decided to take her arm to allow her to spin under him. After she spun, they resumed to the dance they were executing.

After the song ended, the disk jockey was thinking of what to play next. After five seconds, the music resumed. The music of choice was more mellow and relaxing. It started off with acoustic guitars along with calming and uplifting male vocals. Warren and Phoenix were looking each other in the eyes. He could see the light reflecting off of the pupils of her eyes. Her ocean, blue irises became thinner from the dim lights of the dance floor.

Warren and Phoenix smiled, but on this occasion, they were more meaningful. She lifted up her arms and placed them on his shoulders as he placed his arms just above her waist. They began to sway back and forth to match the rhythm and stared at each other.

As one minute passed into the song when the drums came in, Warren and Phoenix engage in conversation, "You want to know something, Phoenix?" Warren said.

"What's that?"

"I'm starting to think of you more as a friend."

"Okay, while we're dancing, let's talk about what we like about each other. Let's start off with you." Warren knew exactly what to say.

"Look at you, you're really beautiful. You're very open-minded, too. You're also one of the only people I actually talked to. I never really talked to anyone, your turn."

"Well, this'll be easy. For one thing, you're strong, and

you're nice. Don't let anyone else think of you differently. It doesn't matter what you've been through, you're still a great man, what else do you like about me? Be honest with me."

"What's more to talk about? You seem to be a perfectly crafted person from the inside since the day I met you." They moved their heads closer to each other as they close their eyes and kiss. A lot of thoughts were going through Warren's mind. Some of the thoughts he was picturing were out of control as he was imagining a future with Phoenix. He's been looking for a second chance ever since the departure of his family. This is the point to one of his most mirthful events of his life.

Warren and Phoenix stopped kissing. They slowly opened their eyes and smiled. "Looks like you win the game," said Phoenix. He immediately, but gently gave her a hug as she did the same with him. Their heads are on top of each other's shoulders. They closed their eyes again and were flattered. They looked at each other face to face, but were still hugging. "I'll never forget this day. Being with you is the best thing I could ever wish for," Warren said. Phoenix's emotions were going out of control as he saw her eyes reflecting more light and her pupils increased in size. "Let's buy a place together."

Warren and Phoenix embraced each other again as she shed a tear on his shoulder. "It's okay, Phoenix, I feel the same way as you do," Warren said before he shed a tear. He gently pat her back to comfort her.

Warren and Phoenix looked at each other face to face. He saw that she was tearing up more. "You alright, Phoenix?" he said, frowning.

"Yeah, I'll be okay." Phoenix was happy and sad.

"What's the matter? You're starting to get a little teary there."

"This is so crazy, Warren. I honestly don't know what to think. I'm just so happy right now, you don't even know." Her heart was beating faster as she was overwhelmed.

"Oh, Phoenix. Don't cry, it'll be alright." Warren lifted his hand up to Phoenix's eye to wipe off her tears and brought back the smile she had. She bent her back forward and set

her head on the center of his chest. He embraced her once

more and closed his eyes. He took his arm off of her and

pulled out his phone. He noticed it was four minutes to

eleven o'clock, which is when the venue closes for the night.

He puts it back in his pocket. "Phoenix," Warren said.

"Yes, Warren?"

"It's about time to go."

"Really? Wow, that was fast," she said cheerfully.

"Yeah, time flies when you're having fun." Phoenix

laughed.

"Amen, to that." They let go of each other and stood side

by side and walked towards the glass doors.

Warren walked up to the door and opened it to allow

Phoenix to walk through. "Why, thank you, Warren!" she said

elatedly.

"You're very welcome, Phoenix!" They walked on the

sidewalk to see Warren's vehicle. He unlocked the car and

opened the doors. They climbed into the vehicle and buckled

their seat belts.

Warren pressed the down arrow of the MENU button until "Navigation" was highlighted. He typed in a new address in the middle of the screen as it was Phoenix's.

Warren put the vehicle into drive. He turned left for the first road of the destination. After driving a hundred and twenty yards, he made a U-turn to enter Allen Street. There were trees off to the sidewalk and had four lanes. "Thank you," said Phoenix.

"No problem, it's what I'm here for," Warren said. The lamps lit up the night brilliantly. Some of the buildings mostly have mirrors to represent their modern appearances as others appeared more historical.

As Warren drove a quarter of a mile, he slowed down to thirty miles per hour. After another quarter of a mile, he stopped to wait for the traffic light to turn green.

As the light flashed green, Warren turned left to enter the street of Broadway. The buildings on Broadway were also historical in appearance.

After a mile of driving on Broadway, Warren stopped and turned left to enter the more suburban side of the city. His left taillight started blinking as he activated his turn signal. He turned on the entrance ramp to enter the highway. The traffic on the highway was more dense than earlier in the day. On his left, he saw the city skyline light up across the horizon.

Warren was driving for eight more miles until he turned left on Phoenix's street. Her street was mostly pitch black with the exception of the dark brown aurora below the horizon.

Warren drove into Phoenix's driveway and set his vehicle in park. Before he had to leave, he looked in her eyes. They smiled at each other one more time. He reached his hand out to gently brush her hair back to show some affection.

Warren and Phoenix kissed. "We'll keep in touch," Warren said. Phoenix slowly opened the passenger door as she looked at him one last time. She climbed out of the car and walked up her porch. He turned his head to see her porch before he put the vehicle in reverse.

Warren kept driving until he was at the end of her

driveway to look for oncoming vehicles. There was a car

approaching, but was far away. He proceeds towards the

highway.

As vehicles were far away from his reach, Warren enters

the highway and continues for the next ten miles. He was

thinking about the night he had with Phoenix.

Chapter 5: Turning Point

June 18, 2014

It was a Wednesday as it approached midday. The skies projected the most beautiful shade of blue as the sunlight shined through the leaves of the trees. There was a house with the brightest shade of white. The house is two stories high with two square windows on each frame of the second floor. The roof had rectangular black shingles with a foot long chimney. The first floor also has square windows. Behind the house were two trees that were a couple feet taller than it. There is a vast piece of farmland with more trees behind the house, forming the shape of a square around it. The driveway is big enough to fit two vehicles pulling in at one time. There were two vehicles in the parking lot, a silver Mercedes-Benz sedan and an orange Pontiac sedan. The vehicles were parked by a white garage with its door closed.

Inside the house was a decoration of tan linoleum flooring with white countertops in the kitchen and a white table towards the center of it. The table was surrounded by metallic chairs that were painted white.

Warren and Phoenix were leaning over the countertop as they kissed. They were wearing white T-shirts and blue denim jeans. "Beautiful day, isn't it?" Warren said.

"It is when you're around." Warren smiled as she smiled back.

"Just wait until later on today, it's going to be more beautiful."

"Looking forward to it."

"My family looks forward to meeting you."

"My family isn't coming," Warren hesitated as he looked down for a brief moment. "Hey," Phoenix said to catch his attention. "Whatever happened years ago happened. Don't let that bother you. As long as we're together, we're okay." He looked into her eyes, but couldn't stop thinking about his childhood. "Trust me," Phoenix calmly said, but firmly. Warren just looked at her, not knowing what to say.

"Okay," he said softly. "Come here," Phoenix said. She gave him a hug as Warren returned the favor. They let go and stood face to face. "Pretty soon, we'll have to get ready for later, I can't keep my mother and father waiting," Phoenix added.

"How much time do we have left?" Phoenix pulled out her phone to check the time. She walked to the staircase behind the table and goes upstairs. She raises her voice, but doesn't yell, "It's about quarter to twelve, the wedding starts at six." Warren was shocked as he lifted his eyes, "Oh, yeah, you're right, we do have to get ready."

Phoenix kept walking upstairs until she set foot on the wood stained hallway floors. She turned the light on to see a hanging light illuminate the entire hallway. She walked to the end of the hallway until she stopped and opened a door beside her as it showed a bedroom. There was a king size bed towards one side of the room. The bedroom has a soft tan carpet floor with beige walls. The mattress of the bed was white along with white blankets with two soft, ivory pillows. She walked around the bed and opened the closet door beside her to reveal her white Contemporary Western wedding dress. The bottom of the dress expanded as she was looking down on it. She walked to the dresser by the bed and opened the drawers to grab a pair of underwear and a bra. She then went to the bathroom across the bedroom and closed the bathroom door.

Phoenix undressed herself to take a shower. She slid open the glass door of the shower cabinet and turned on the water. Inside the shower were two hubs with one on each side. The water started raining down as she waited for it to get warmer a few seconds later. The temperature of the water caused the shower to be filled with steam as she was letting the water rain down on her body.

After fifteen minutes, Phoenix opened the shower

cabinet. The steam escaped onto the ceiling. She stepped out

to open the pantry door beside her. She grabbed a towel to

gently dry herself off. She started to put on the straps of her

bra along with her underwear.

Phoenix grabbed her red toothbrush with white accents

from a drawer below the sink. She grabbed a tube of

toothpaste out of the drawer and continued squeezing until it

touched all bristles and started brushing her teeth. She then

grabbed the bar of soap to wash her hands. She moved her

hands over the water to rinse and dried her hands off.

Phoenix went into the bedroom to grab her white blouse

hanging from the closet and bent down to grab her white

high heels. She grabbed her wedding dress and gently placed

it on the bed. She went back to the closet and grabbed the

hose and pulled both pieces up to her legs. She inserted the

white garters around the hose to hold them up in place.

Warren was in the other bathroom from the opposite

side of the bedroom. He was just getting out of the shower to put his underwear and dress socks on and brushed his teeth. He exited the bathroom and walked to the bedroom.

Warren and Phoenix decided to not follow the tradition of the groom not seeing the bride before the wedding, since they lived together for two years. Warren saw that Phoenix was trying to put on the first piece of her dress. He took out his navy blue suit jacket and bowtie, red boutonnière, black dress pants, white vest and dress shirt out of the closet. After he put his shirt and jacket on, Phoenix stepped into the sparkling silver silhouette of her dress. She pulled it up until it was at the top of her chest. She then took the bottom part of her dress and stepped her legs into it, but she was struggling. "Here, let me help you with that," Warren said.

"Please?" Phoenix said as she was laughing. "You might have to sit on the side of the bed in order for this to kind of work," he insisted.

"Okay, I will do that." Phoenix gently sat on the bed. Warren set the bottom part of her dress on the other side of where she's sitting. He took it and inserted it through her legs. As Phoenix's legs were in the bottom piece, she waited for the next step. "You can stand up now," he said. He was trying to hold the back up against her body. He added, "And after that, it looks like there's a button you need to clip on the center of your waist." The bottom was up to her hips as she clipped the button. She slowly walked around to see if it'll stay, and it did. "Yay! It stays!" Phoenix said with joy and humor. Warren pulled up his dress pants and put on his dress shoes. "I might need your help again, need to put on my high heels," she said.

"Sure, I can do that." Warren grabbed her high heels out of the closet and slid her feet into them.

Warren grabbed his bowtie as he tried to put it on himself, but had a hard time doing it. He lifted up his collar and draped the tie over his neck. The ends of the tie crossed at the same length towards each other. He crossed the ends of the tie and looped one end over the other, but it didn't look right. He has never worn a bowtie before. "I don't think that's on right," Phoenix pointed out.

"Yeah, can you help me with this, please?"

"Here, let me help you." Phoenix walked up to him and lifted her arms up to his neck. "Okay, here, let me show you something." She unlooped the tie until she grabbed a hold of both ends. "You have to have one of the ends about a couple inches over the other." She buttoned the top of Warren's shirt. She pulled one of the ends of the tie down on his left side and crossed both of the ends' lengths, forming an X. "And then you loop it over." She brings the longer end of the tie behind the shorter one as she passed it through the loop. The longer end is now hanging over the shorter one. She adjusted the bowtie closer to his neck. "Is that too tight?" she questioned.

"No, it's good."

"Okay, but if it gets too tight, let me know."

"Alright."

"Now, you double the short end." Phoenix pushed the long end of the tie aside and doubled the other onto itself, forming a knot. She brought the smaller part of the short end up to the knot as it was lined up with both collar points.

"Line this up behind the bow," Phoenix said while talking to herself. She held the bow and pulled the longer end while lining it up straight behind the bow. "Loop it around." She looped it around in the middle of the bow. "You push this in the center." She gently shook the bow to get Warren's attention. She pushed the wide center of the longer end through the bow's knot. It created another bow, which was facing the opposite direction of the bow she made earlier.

"Tighten these up," Phoenix concluded. She pulled on both of the bows to tighten the knot. She gently pulled on the ends to their original length. For the finishing touches, she straightened the knot. "Thank you," Warren said. She got close to his face while making a flirtatious smirk. She said while whispering, "You helped me before, so I'm returning the favor." They kissed and looked at each other. Warren then crouched down to tie his dress shoes. "Well, don't you look handsome?" Phoenix said flirtatiously.

"And don't you look beautiful?"

Phoenix grabbed her tiara and went to the bathroom to fix her hair and grabbed a comb from the sink. She wetted her hair and combed it to make nice and fine, straight creases. She combed the back of her hair and rolled a patch of it backwards. Her tiara was made of diamonds with the shapes of flowers around it. She grabbed a bottle of hairspray from the pantry and sprayed whiffs around her hair. She placed her tiara in the middle as it locked into place to prevent the back of her hair from collapsing. She walked into the bedroom to find the translucent head gown in her closet.

Warren went to the bathroom beside the bedroom to fix his hair. He grabbed a comb from the drawer and grabbed a bottle of hair mousse from the pantry. He wets his hair in order for the mousse to provide maximum effect. He shook the bottle vigorously and squeezed some out as it made a bubbling and whistling sound. Phoenix smiled as she raised her eyebrow and laughed. Warren smiled, "What? That's what mousse does for you."

"Yeah, but the sound of it though."

"I think it's just this brand." Phoenix still laughed for a few seconds until she sighed.

"Oh, Warren," she said joyfully.

Warren gently rubbed the mousse together and applied it to his hair. He combed until all of it was sticking up. He then combed it sideways to see that all of it was lined straight up. He then applied men's hairspray for the finishing touches.

Phoenix walked to the mirror above the dresser to make sure she's putting on her head gown correctly. She gently placed it over the top of her head and pulled it to the back of her hair. The length of the head gown was about six feet long.

Warren went in the bedroom to stand beside Phoenix. He noticed that the flowers from the vase by the bedroom's window were gone. Phoenix was carrying a handful of red roses as the sunlight shined behind her. They smiled. Warren chuckled, but not in humor, but as a way of admiring her. He wrapped his arm around her shoulder to show some affection. He was slowly rubbing his hand over her shoulder. Phoenix leaned her head over his shoulder while closing her eyes. He moved his head over to kiss Phoenix in the forehead.

While admiring each other, Warren and Phoenix heard the purr of a vehicle's engine. "Is someone here?" Phoenix said.

"Sounds like it, let's go see who it is." They proceeded to walk downstairs side by side. "Be careful," said Warren, warning her not to fall down the steps in her high heels.

Upon opening the two glass doors, Warren left them open for Phoenix to get through without getting stuck between them. "Thank you," said Phoenix.

"Mm-hmm," Warren nodded as they walk down the porch steps. The skies showed no sign of clouds as the sun made Phoenix's dress more vibrant.

Warren and Phoenix see a white stretch Chrysler 300 limousine parked in front of their vehicles. Its wheels have five spoke rims with a chrome finish. It resembled the badge of the SRT8 edition from the Chrysler 300 lineup. The bumper has a black grille in the center with a chrome lining with its emblem engraved in it. They were amazed by the overall appearance of the limousine.

The driver of the limousine opened his door and stood on their sidewalk. He was white in skin color. He has black hair straightened like Warren's and was wearing sunglasses. He was wearing a red suit jacket over a black dress shirt along with black dress pants and dress shoes of the same color. The driver walked up to him to shake his hand. "Hello, how are you doing this evening?" the driver said.

"Pretty well, how about yourself, sir?" Warren said.

"Pretty good, not to mention the gorgeous weather outside."

"Yeah, I know, right?" Warren and Phoenix laugh, including the driver. The driver then walked over to Phoenix, "Hello, ma'am, how are you today?" Phoenix put her flowers on one hand to shake the driver's hand.

"Good and excited." Phoenix held the flowers with both of her hands as the driver gave his instructions. "For today, I will be your driver throughout the duration of your wedding," the driver said. A woman opened the passenger door and climbed out of the limousine. The driver didn't notice until he looked behind him to see her in a sparkling red dress with red high heels. The woman has blonde hair as her head was long and her body was slender. She was holding a black photography camera. The driver introduced the woman, "Oh, and she will be one of the main photographers taking pictures throughout your wedding. She will be taking your pictures right now."

"How are you two doing this afternoon?" the photographer said.

"Pretty good," Warren and Phoenix said.

"Where would you like your picture taken?"

"Oh, we never talked about that," Phoenix said quietly to herself and to Warren. They hesitated for a moment to figure out where to get their picture. "Take your time," the photographer said.

"Umm.....we want a picture of a close up of us with the house. We also want a shot with our vehicles in the driveway," Phoenix said.

"Okay." The photographer smiled and walked backwards until she was standing in front of the limousine. "Walk up to where the camera is, and I'll let you know when to stop."

Warren and Phoenix smiled as they were walking towards the photographer.

"And, stop." The photographer could see Warren and Phoenix standing beside each other with their house and vehicles behind them. The photographer took a few steps forward to get closer to them, "Okay, now smile." The photographer pressed the flash button to take a picture. "Okay, now what I want you guys to do is to stand with both your legs together while facing each other."

Warren and Phoenix looked into the camera. "Aww, look at you two, you guys look cute together," the photographer complimented. "Okay, now smile for the camera." They smiled with their teeth out as the camera flashed.

After the photographer was done, the driver directed Warren and Phoenix to the limousine. "Okay, if you guys follow behind me, I'll show you where to sit in the back of the vehicle," the driver said. "Right this way." Warren and Phoenix were right behind him. They continued walking until they were standing by the middle of the limousine. All of the windows were tinted black on both sides. The driver politely opened the car door for them. "Feel free to explore the interior of the vehicle," said the driver.

"Thank you!" they said.

Warren and Phoenix climbed into the interior and saw black, stitched leather seats beside them. The leather seats mimicked a couch as they were fused together. The carpet on the floor was black as it was woven in texture. Towards the back of the limousine, there were seats big enough for two people.

Warren and Phoenix sat on the leather seats. The driver closed the door behind them. As they looked straight, there was a built-in radio with a glossed wooden countertop to support it. Beside the radio was another row of seats fused together. They were big enough for about three people. On the ceiling was a mirror that extended across the back seats.

They smiled in awe and looked around to explore the interior.

"Wow, this interior is nice!" Phoenix said.

"Yeah, this is actually pretty nice for a first-timer in a limousine."

"What do you mean by that?"

"This is my first time entering a limousine."

"Yeah, same here." Warren and Phoenix smiled at each other. He said, "I'm glad I get to spend the whole day with you. One of my dreams are finally coming true. Getting to spend a lifetime with a woman like you."

"Especially with a man that has a good heart." They kissed.

Warren and Phoenix felt the limousine go backwards and started going down the road. After the limousine took a left, he was driving through roads filled with two-story houses on both sides. The driver made another left to be surrounded by trees. The trees were tall enough to fill the road with shadows.

After a half of a mile of driving, the driver was able to

see another part of town, but with fewer houses. He slowed down and turned into the parking lot at a local chapel. The parking lot was already filled with vehicles by the time they pulled in. Warren pulled out his phone to check the time as it was four o'clock in the afternoon. He then turned it off.

"We're here," said the driver. The driver came around the limousine to let Warren and Phoenix out. "You ready?" Warren said to Phoenix.

"Ready when you are," she said. They walked out with Phoenix going first. The driver was still standing by the car door as Warren got out. They walked side by side as they were in between two parked vehicles and see the front entrance doors to the chapel.

As Warren and Phoenix approached the entrance doors, there were two doormen holding them for invited guests. Both of the doormen were white in skin color as one of them had black hair and the other had blonde hair. Both of them were wearing business attire. There were two lines of bushes that formed an upside-down L-shape in between the doors spaced from each other in a reflected pattern.

Warren and Phoenix walked in the chapel to see a hallway with tan walls and flooring. The floor was rather clean as it shined from the ceiling lights. They noticed two police officers by the doors with one on each side. They were wearing light blue uniform shirts with the badge of the New York City Police Department on their chests.

Phoenix was confused of where to go. "Umm.....do you know where the dressing rooms are?" she said to one of the officers.

"It's all the way on the left," the officer said. Warren and Phoenix walked towards the far end of the hallway. There were two separate doors with dressing rooms for men and women. They looked at each other and smiled before entering the dressing rooms.

After about two hours of passing, Warren and Phoenix walked into the hallway. Phoenix has her white head gown hung over in front of her face and held the roses. They continued walking until they entered a room filled with people. The room was surrounded by white walls and brown, wooden benches. The room was about fifty feet from the front entrance.

The composition for Here Comes The Bride immediately started playing. The piece was accompanied by people playing the trumpets and violins. The aisle has a red carpet. There were stained windows of Christian reference on both sides of the room. Some of the windows had reference to the Virgin Mary as the rest depicted Jesus Christ.

All of the people looked at Warren and Phoenix and smiled as all of them were dressed up. Warren and Phoenix smiled as they walked closer to the small steps and saw a priest by a white arch ahead of them. The arch was decorated with various colors and flowers around it. The priest was holding a bible that was dark brown in color. The priest was an older man as he ranged in his fifties and has gray hair. He was wearing a white gown with a red sash hanging around his neck.

As Warren and Phoenix walked towards the arch, the

ceremony began. The priest took a moment to clear his throat before he spoke, "We are gathered here today for this day of joy. We are gathered to share a moment with Warren Leyton and Phoenix Hadaway as they exchange their vows of their everlasting love." They were smiling as the priest gave his speech. "We are honored to witness the joyous love of a new family. A family that will be nourished and nurtured through the devotion of two individuals growing through the bonds of life. May their marriage bring them peace, joy, comfort, and fulfillment that is known in the hearts of God's children. An essential of an honorable marriage is a substantial bond of friendship and trust."

Phoenix put her head down to briefly look at the floor. The priest continued, "After every passing day, your love for each other will continue to grow as each moment passes. Warren and Phoenix, it's important to remember that your love for each other will stand on a foundation of pure, mutual affection and respect for each other." They looked at each other firmly. "To love another person is to be willing to accept their strong points, and their weak points, with equal measures of understanding and respect."

Warren and Phoenix were asked to take each other's hands to finish the ceremony. The priest looked at Warren, "Do you, Warren, take Phoenix as your one and true love?"

"I do." The priest looked at Phoenix, "And do you, Phoenix, take Warren as your one and only true love?"

"I do."

"Anyone speak now or forever hold your peace." There was a moment of silence, but no hands were raised. "I now pronounce you husband and wife. You may now kiss the bride." Warren and Phoenix smiled as they hugged and kissed. The audience smiled and clapped in joy. "I now pronounce you, Mr. and Mrs. Leyton," the priest concluded.

Warren and Phoenix walked down the aisle and exited the worship room. The composition of the Wedding March began playing. They kept walking until they were outside. Phoenix saw her parents walk out of the chapel. Her mother had blonde hair with sunglasses and was in her fifties. She was wearing a yellow overcoat with yellow dress and high heels. Her father has black hair while also wearing sunglasses and a black overcoat and was in his fifties. He was also wearing black dress pants with black dress shoes. "Phoenix!" her mother said. Her mother walked up to her and give her a hug. Phoenix laughed in joy.

"Hey, mom! I'd like you to meet my husband, Warren."

"Hey, Warren, nice to meet you." Phoenix's mother shook his hand.

"Nice to meet you, too," Warren said. Phoenix's father looked at him and shook his hand. "Hello there, Warren, it's nice to meet you. You seem like a nice guy, Phoenix has been talking a lot about you lately," Phoenix's father said. Warren and Mr. Hadaway stopped shaking hands.

"She's my only one, too," Warren said.

"You're the first one to actually date her and marry her, too. Hope you treat her good."

"I will, sir, cross my heart and my will to die."

"That's what I like to hear, because in a world like this,

people need some love here and there."

"Amen to that," Warren said as he laughed, but understood his seriousness. Warren looked at Phoenix and kissed her. They walk back to the limousine to prepare for their wedding party.

"I'll see you later, Mom!" Phoenix said, waving goodbye to her mother.

"Bye, I'll see you at the reception hall!" The couple sat down and started hugging and kissing as the limousine drove out of the parking lot. The vehicle was hanging turns in both directions as it was leaving the couple's hometown.

After driving for a mile, the driver then entered the highway. The highway was densely packed with vehicles. The vehicle accelerated to match the vehicles' speed beside him. The skies were projecting its natural beauty as the couple saw the orangish-yellow glare projected by the sun. "Thank you," Warren said to Phoenix after he kissed her. "For everything."

"Anything for you, baby," she said as her eyes were closed. They kissed. After three miles of driving, the driver entered an exit ramp on the right.

Warren and Phoenix noticed that they were now in the downtown area of New York City. The driver made his way in one of the more open and spacious areas of the city.

The vehicle pulled into the parking lot of a ballroom. In the parking entrance, there was a building with two glass entrance doors that were eight feet tall. The exterior of the ballroom was white in color. There was a red neon sign on top of the building. The parking lot was filled with vehicles ranging from various sports cars, sports utility vehicles, and luxury vehicles. The parking lot was big enough to fit four hundred vehicles.

The limousine pulled into the parking lot as the driver saw two parking spaces. The couple climbed out of the vehicle and were standing beside each other as they walked on the sidewalk of the ballroom. Warren pulled open one of the entrance doors to let Phoenix through.

"Thank you," Phoenix said to Warren and winked as she walked in. He smiled. The ceiling of the ballroom was decorated with cream white tiles and lights hanging from golden chains in groups of three. There were round tables with white tablecloths over top of them that looked fresh and clean. Each of the tables were big enough to fit at least eight people. The aisle in the center had thin white lines that separated the tables on both sides. The aisle stretched to forty feet in width. Towards the end of the aisle was a table with ten dining chairs with cushions made out of soft, white fur. The table was decorated with two vases of flowers in the center.

The ballroom was already filled with people as they screamed and clapped, congratulating them. Everyone looked at the couple and smiled as they walked in. Warren wanted to say something to his wife before they decided to run up the aisle, "Hey, Phoenix."

"Yeah."

"You ready for this?"

"Ready when you are. I was born ready." Dance music started playing as they were running to the table ahead of them. The music was composed of electronic sawtooth

synths and percussion that was rich and punchy in bass.

There was an announcer standing by the aisle with a wireless

microphone.

Warren and Phoenix walked to the announcer to shake

his hand. The announcer was a man with skin color that was a

mix of brown and tan. He has black hair that reflected from

the lights of the room's interior. He was wearing a black suit

jacket with a white dress shirt and a black tie under it. He was

also wearing black dress pants and shoes. "Hey,

congratulations, you guys, you earned it!" the announcer

said. He was shaking their hands before speaking into the

microphone. The couple turned their heads towards each

other and smiled. The announcer spoke through the

microphone, "And here are the newlyweds, Warren and

Phoenix! Everybody give them a big round of applause!"

The crowd of people clapped and screamed in joy. Some

of the crowd was standing instead of sitting. All of the people

attending were formally dressed with various colors of suit

jackets from the men and dresses from the women. The announcer continued speaking, but Phoenix wanted to say something. The announcer said, "Before we start the party tonight, Phoenix has something to say to her friends and family! Phoenix, take it away!" The announcer handed the microphone to her.

"Thank you," she said before speaking into the microphone.

"You're welcome," the announcer said quietly.

"Hello everyone," Phoenix paused to think as she looked down on the floor. "I would like to thank all of my family and friends for coming out for this wonderful event. I would like to introduce my husband, Warren!" The audience clapped and yelled in joy as Warren waved to everyone. "I'm glad that I married this man because we learned a lot from each other in the past two years," she paused again and shed a tear. "Without him........, I would have never felt the same. He's always been there for me since the day I met him. Every day, our love gets stronger as every moment passes by." Warren was standing by her as he also shed a tear. "I am honored to see all of the people that gathered here today as we celebrate friendship and the everlasting effect of love. Thank you!"

Phoenix handed the microphone back to the announcer. "Alright, everybody, before we get started with the party, I would like everybody to bow their heads as we make a prayer for tonight," the announcer said. Everyone bowed their heads as they waited for the prayer, including Warren and Phoenix. "Lord, we thank you for this gathering of people for the night. We thank you for giving these people the chance to be with their friends and family as we celebrate the moments of love and friendship. From this day forward, we will continue to learn as we walk on the fine soils of our beautiful home. We would like to thank you for letting us celebrate a moment of joy that's ahead of us for tonight. Amen."

"Amen!" the crowd shouted out. The couple hugged and kissed.

"Aw," the crowd said.

The music resumed playing as the couple sat down at their table. The music of choice was rhythm and blues music. The synthesized voices and the electronic symphony were flowing together with the rhythmic percussive hits.

The rhythm got people pumped up for dancing. Some of the people rushed up to the dance floor as they were already moving rhythmically to the music. To some of the more enthusiastic people, they started to do the jitterbug, which is a type of swing dance that originated in the twentieth century.

Warren and Phoenix rushed to the dance floor. They set their hands on each other's arms and danced to the rhythm. They were dancing the same way back when Warren surprised her from Del Posto. "Hmm, just like old times, huh?" Warren said.

"Brings back old memories," Phoenix said flirtatiously to him.

After thirty minutes of dancing, the couple noticed that there were chefs coming out while holding trays with sheets of aluminum foil covering over their tops, containing various kinds of food. They set the trays down on a table to the far side of the ballroom. The table was vast as it stretched to the other side. The table was big enough for sixty different trays of food. There were candles that were lit up on both ends of the table. Some of the people have already lined up to wait for their food.

Warren and Phoenix were the first in line as the line of people was quickly getting filled behind them. Warren was behind Phoenix. "This sure brings back old memories," he said. Phoenix turned around to face Warren.

"Yep, it sure does." They laughed and kissed.

Warren and Phoenix saw one of the first trays presented on the table. There were various plates and napkins next to it. The tray contained pieces of rotisserie chicken with a pair of tongs. They grabbed a plate and some napkins. As the line shrunk halfway down the table, Phoenix scooped some peas and mashed potatoes with the spoons by the middle of the trays. "Wow, there is so much food! So many choices, I do not know where to start!" Phoenix said.

"Yeah, I don't know what to choose from either!" They laughed as they were filling their plates. As they walked towards the end of the trays of food, there was a small table that held various brands of soft drinks packaged in two-liter bottles. They walked to their table and set their plates down at the center. They went to the other side of the room to a bar that serves various exotic brands of wine and liquor.

As Warren and Phoenix were standing in front of the bar, there was a young female bartender wiping the glasses using a white, soft towel for serving customers. She had blonde hair and was wearing a black suit jacket with a black dress shirt and was white in skin color. "Hey, guys, congratulations on your wedding," the bartender said in a friendly voice.

"Thank you," Phoenix said.

"Thank you very much," Warren said. They looked behind the bartender to see the bottles of alcohol.

"You guys are very welcome, now how can I help you two tonight?"

"Um....I'll take a glass of red Merlot wine if you have that kind," Warren said.

"Yes, we sure do and what can I get for you, ma'am?"

"Um....I'll take the same as my husband."

"Okay, I will get right on that." The couple patiently waited for their drinks as they put their arms around each other's waist. After waiting, the bartender came up to the counter with two wine glasses of Merlot.

"Okay, if you want any more food and drinks of any kind, feel free to get what you want. I'll always be up here if you need any refills. So yeah, guys, enjoy your evening. It's your night, so make the best of it."

"We're already up on that," Warren said as he looked at Phoenix.

"I can tell," the bartender said, smiling. The couple turned around and walked back to their table. On Warren's dish was smoked salmon, mashed potatoes with gravy, an ear of sweet corn, and some roast beef. "You sure do love your beef," Phoenix said. Warren looked at her and smiled.

After the couple was done eating, the announcer came with his microphone. The music stopped immediately. "Okay, may I have everyone's attention, please? Everybody return to their tables," the announcer said. People sat back at their tables, but some were still standing. "How's everybody doing this evening?" The crowd cheered as they yelled across the room. "Alright! That's what I like to hear! Now here's what we're going to do. A wedding party's not a party without cake, right?"

The kitchen door opened as there were two butlers carrying a steel cart with a white, seven layer wedding cake. "So, here's what we're going to do, the butlers are going to serve the cake, but there's a catch," the announcer hinted. The couple became anxious. "They're going to have a cake fight!"

The butlers sliced a piece of cake off of its bottom layer with triangular spatulas. They crouched down to the bottom of the cart to grab two plates. They gently slid the pieces of cake off of the spatulas and served them to the couple.

Warren and Phoenix break off a piece of their cake and brought them to each other's mouth. They were about to take a bite. Right before Warren was about to clamp his teeth down on Phoenix's piece, she smeared the cake on his face. Most of his face was covered with cake and icing. The audience was laughing humorously as they saw his face. Warren could smell the cake on his face.

The audience payed attention as Warren was about to feed Phoenix. He smeared the cake on her face to return the favor. They smiled as they hugged and kissed. For the next two hours, the music resumed playing as everybody ran up to the dance floor including Warren and Phoenix.

The music paused as the announcer picked up his microphone, "Is everybody having a good time?" The crowd applauded as they shouted. "Well, it's about time to pack up because it's about five minutes before the party's over, but we'll squeeze out one more song. This time, we're going to take things slow."

The music resumed playing as it started with calm female

vocals. There were also swinging percussive hits and the beautiful melodies of acoustic guitars. Warren placed his hands on Phoenix's hips as she placed her hands on his shoulders. They were swaying back and forth to the rhythm. They looked into each other's eyes as they were smiling. "Just like the good old times, Phoenix," Warren said.

"I'll remember this night," Phoenix said. "For the rest of my life." They kissed right before the song ended.

"Okay, everybody, give one last round of applause for the newlyweds," the announcer said as the crowd cheered. "Have a good night!"

Everybody walked towards the glass doors to exit the ballroom. Warren and Phoenix held each other's hands. They looked at each other as they still had icing on their faces. They looked up at the obsidian skies to see the stars light up the night. The couple walked to the limousine as the driver was standing by his seat, waiting for the couple. The driver opened the doors for them. Warren allowed Phoenix to climb in first as he followed her. The driver closed the door as soon as the couple sat down and buckled their seat belts.

After waiting for the road to clear up, he proceeded to

drive the newlyweds home.

Chapter 6: Recruit

July 7, 2017

Over the passing years, technology has been advancing

drastically. The interior of the elevator was completely

redesigned. They were upgraded to increase efficiency and

productivity throughout the workplace. The mirrored walls

were removed as they were replaced by walls with the color

of cream white. The walls and the ceiling were translucent as

Warren could see his reflection around him. The edges of the

walls were black in color. The lighting of the ceiling was just as

bright from the previous years, but the light bulbs have been

replaced. They have been reduced to two light bulbs in

the shape of tubes. The touchpads were also different. The colors of the displays have changed to neon green as well as the up and down arrows as they were embedded.

After the elevator opened, Warren walked to the counter of the lobby booth. The exterior touchpads were the same as the elevator's interior. The lobby room was nearly empty. He looked behind him to see only a couple people walking around. He was working the night shift on a warm, Friday night. The room was more up to date as the years passed by. The ceiling lights were brighter as the walls were their brightest shade of white. Beside the glass entrance doors were bushes topped with freshly planted lavenders and blues.

Warren lifted up his office equipment bag as the strap was about to fall off of his shoulder. He turned around to face the woman working behind the counter. She has blonde hair with a black T-shirt, bearing the company's name. Instead of a clipboard, there was a machine with a six-inch digital black screen clipped on the side of the counter for signing out.

There was a black stylus pen clipped beside the screen. He slid out the stylus pen to sign his name. The screen changed to a light green color as he was writing his signature. "You have a good day, ma'am," he said politely.

"You, too, sir!" the woman said.

As Warren walked to the glass doors, they slid apart as they disappeared into the walls. The doors reappeared after he walked onto the sidewalk. The building's exterior went through some redesigning as well. The company's logo remained in the same place, but it was embedded. The logo was different as there was a custom-made ampersand between the B and the N. The typeface of the word, "Financing" was serif and italicized in style, similar to what Warren made. The walls of the building had different material as it was composed of steel.

Warren was waiting to cross the road. The common commuters were becoming less frequent. The vehicles were replaced by numerous sports cars and luxury vehicles. The production of high-performance vehicles were increasing in productivity at this time. They became more common on

commercial and city roads. The vehicles that are slowly

passing by were all vibrant in color as they came closer to his

way.

After waiting, Warren crossed to the other side. Vehicles

were coming from both directions, but they were a tenth of a

mile away. The street lamps were lit up brilliantly as the light

reflected onto the pavement. He looked up into the obsidian

skies to see the waxing of the crescent moon. The stars

showed irregular patterns as they lit up the sky.

Warren's skin felt cooler as he walked into the shadows

of the trees under him. He took a deep and relieving breath

and walked straight.

Warren walked to the entrance of Parking Garage A. The

entrance and exit signs were different as the fencing went

through a makeover as well. There were thick doors and walls

that were composed of massive steel bolts made in rows for

upgraded security. There was an electronic security lock

system installed throughout the grounds of the parking

garages. He saw a touchpad with the same layout as a phone. Its display emitted neon green lights while showing numbers in black. There was a text box above it. Employees and staff members have to type in their work identification number, which is a seven-digit code to enter the lot.

Warren typed in his WIN as he quickly jumped from one number to another. He heard the clicking of the bolts as they were unlocking and slowly moved into the wall. They made a continuous and loud whistling noise as Warren walked into the lot. The whistling stopped as they disappeared into the wall. There was a small flight of four steps that replaced the slant. It was made of cement and was painted tan. As he walked up the steps, the steel bolts reappeared and closed behind him as he walked away.

As Warren was walking, he turned his head to see the lot. There were only about twenty vehicles. He walked to the left to notice the entrance of the parking garage.

Warren walked to the right to walk up the small steps to enter the garage. The lighting was brand new as it was replaced by fluorescent tubing. There was a sign that was replaced by a four-foot digital display projecting the number, 1. The digital display was blood-red in color.

As Warren walked to the left, he noticed that the slanted ramps haven't changed. Once he entered the third floor, he noticed there was another vehicle that looked exactly like his Mercedes-Benz.

Warren walked down the small steps to get to his car. "Warren!" a man's voice called out his name.

Warren was shocked as he looked around. He noticed a black man leaning up against a wall by the guardrail dressed in formal attire with his arms crossed. He wore all black except for his white dress shirt. "It is *so* nice to meet you," the man said in a cocky voice.

"Who the hell are you, and how do you know my name?"

"Remember the time that I looked at you on the road a few years back?" Warren was getting frustrated.

"Yeah, what about it? And first of all, who are you?!"

"The name's Barrett. Barrett Atkinson." Barrett got off of the wall and slowly walked towards Warren. "Now, you seem like a smart man. I'm intrigued by your performance in the business, is that correct?"

"And how do you know where I work, have you been following me?"

"I got a job for you, Warren."

"Well, it was nice talking to you, but I'm not interested in your damn job. Don't follow me again." He turned his back and walked away from Barrett. Barrett got frustrated after he refused the offer. He sprints like the speed of an Olympic runner after Warren.

Barrett grinned his teeth with his eyes wide open and yelled in rage. Warren turned his back just before Barrett tackled him to the ground. He grunted as Barrett pinned him down. Warren was scared, not knowing what's going to happen next. Barrett clenched his fists and charged them at Warren's head. Barrett punched his face as his head jerked from the intense velocity of the punch. Warren was helpless as his arms were pinned from Barrett's knees. His nose started to bruise with blood coming out profusely. "Please!! Stop!! Somebody help me!!" Warren begged for mercy as the rest of his face was getting bruised. He almost received a black eye as the closest damage from his eyes was both of his cheekbones.

After fifteen seconds of beating, Barrett let Warren go, but not for long. He quickly got up on his feet and ran away from Barrett. Warren was feeling dizzy. Barrett charged at him once more. He fiercely pushed Warren onto a wall near a well-lit fluorescent light. They were standing about a couple feet from the light source.

Barrett resumed as he started flying fists and kicks onto Warren's body. He punched him in his diaphragm, causing him to bend forward. Warren made a raspy cough and pressed his hands against his diaphragm. Barrett kicked the bottom of his chin and performed a left hook on his cheek. He then continued to punch him in his diaphragm.

Warren was feeling weak at this point. His whole body

was swaying in a dizzy state. Barrett executed a swift kick,

causing Warren to slam to the ground. He was laying helpless

while grunting in pain. He was still coughing, but sounded

weaker and more hoarse. Barrett slowly walked up to Warren

as he was backing away from him.

Barrett crouched down and ferociously grabbed Warren

by his suit jacket and dress shirt. He was still coughing as

Barrett had him in his tight grip. Barrett walked at a fast pace

as he was holding him. He pushed Warren back onto the spot

near the lights. Barrett's face was a few inches from Warren's

as he gave him a furious look. Barrett widened his eyes and

pressed his lips together. Warren could feel the air coming

out of Barrett's nose. He was finally able to breathe, but was

suffering from the whiplash as he was hyperventilating. The

light was shining on their faces. Barrett said in an enraged

voice, but didn't yell, "You listen to me, and YOU listen to me

good, alright?! Now you're going to do what I say from here

on out!"

"What..... do.... you..... want.... from.... me?" Warren said in his weak and hoarse voice.

"I don't give a damn what you do, or what you want, or what you have!" He was building pressure onto Warren's chest and pressed his hand against him. "Join me," Barrett said. "Join me in an effort to tear down the very fabrics of our society. I will hunt down the next person I choose no matter what it takes and I will stop at nothing to finish the job."

"You're...... just.. like....... my.. father. Not...... giving.... a.... damn..... about..... nobody..... but... himself."

"Yeah, well sometimes the truth hurts. Deal with it!" Barrett shifted his eyes down and pulled out his cell phone from his pocket, "I see that you're married. You got a beautiful looking wife. It would be terrible to see something bad happen to her, right?" Warren gave Barrett a disgusted look as he showed no remorse. "You think about it," Barrett concluded.

Barrett let go of Warren, but he wasn't able to get on his feet. He fell to the ground and moaned in pain. Barrett was walking away from him as he was walking to his sedan. He opened the door and climbed into his vehicle and drove off.

Warren attempted to get up, but struggled in doing so. He started to lift himself off from the ground as he was grunting from the pain. He stood on the ground and started limping as he took a couple steps. He had to walk the thirty feet to his vehicle, but it felt like a mile to him. Almost every time he moves his right leg, he grunts.

Warren tried to pull his car keys out as his arms were shaking feverishly. His right arm was shaking even more as he inserted the key into the back door of his vehicle. He made an effort to pull off the strap of his equipment bag and set it in the back seats. He closed the back door and walked to the driver's side. His arms were still shaky, but not as much after he took off his equipment bag. He unlocked the door and climbed into the vehicle. He felt dazed as he lazily sat on the seat and set his keys over the dashboard. He puts his head down with his eyes closed and took a couple deep breaths before closing the door.

After recollecting himself, he pulled out his phone to call

Phoenix. He was scared to death at this point. The time reads as quarter to nine o'clock. He dialed their house phone number and placed his phone over his ear.

Phoenix was sleeping at the time. She opened her eyes as she heard the house phone ring in the kitchen. She pushed the blanket off of her and crawled out of bed. She walked at a fast pace into the hallway. The phone was still ringing as she walked downstairs.

As Phoenix entered the kitchen, she walked to the countertop to grab a black wireless phone. She was wearing a plain red T-shirt and a pair of black underwear. She pressed the TALK button, "Hello?" Warren tried to speak a word out of his mouth.

"Phoenix........," he said.

"Warren? Are you okay?" Phoenix was starting to get worried.

"I've..... been... beaten up."

"What?! Are you serious?!"

"Some.... man...... beat.. me.... up...., but.... I'm.. still......

able... to... drive." Warren's lower body wasn't as damaged as his upper body.

"Are you sure?"

"Yes....., Phoenix."

"Okay, call me back if there are any problems. Please be extra careful on the road," she said. "I love you."

"I... love you, too."

"I'll see you when you get home. I'll be in the kitchen waiting for you."

"Alright. I'll.... see you.... in... a little.... bit. Bye."

"Bye." Phoenix pressed the DISMISS button and put the phone back to its original place. She pulled a chair out from the table and tried to think of possible scenarios of why someone would do bodily harm to Warren. "What the hell happened?" Phoenix said to herself.

Warren placed the phone back in his pocket. He grabbed the keys off of the dashboard to start his vehicle and set it in reverse. He was still slightly dazed as he faced one of the support beams. He tapped the throttle and straightened the vehicle until he faced the digital display of an exit sign. It was

embedded into the wall as he looked straight.

Warren accelerated to ten miles per hour. He stopped

and turned left to enter the downward ramp to switch floors.

He took a deep breath as his diaphragm was stinging and

started grunting.

Warren drove out of the parking garage and headed

straight to the steel bolts in the lot. He stopped to wait for

the bolts to open.

Warren noticed the buildings lighting up the city. The

engine roared as he accelerated to forty-five miles per hour.

Warren wiped his face down with his hand to wake himself

up from the dizziness. He was starting to get nervous, "What

the hell just happened?" he said to himself. He stopped to

make a right to enter the highway. His respiratory rate was

going faster as he propelled to sixty-five miles per hour. By

the time he reached that speed, his breathing slowed down.

The density of vehicles was close to minimal, buying him

some extra time to drive home.

"Come on, Warren, where could you be?" Phoenix said as she was still sitting at the kitchen table. She covered her hands over her face as she was still worried. Warren continued driving straight for the next fifteen miles on the highway.

Warren stopped to turn right to enter the street of their house. All of the houses were two stories high. He stopped pulled into their driveway as he saw Phoenix's sedan.

Warren slowly opened the car door and climbed out to set foot on the driveway. He closed the door and walked on the curved sidewalk to their porch while struggling to keep his pace. He walked up the porch steps as Phoenix heard him.

Phoenix rushed to the door to open it for Warren. She was shocked and scared to see the damage on his body. "Oh, no, Warren!" Phoenix grabbed him to prevent him from falling on the floor. "Are you okay?" Phoenix gently rubbed his back to comfort him. She panicked, thinking of what to do. "Come on, come with me, let's get you cleaned up." She wrapped her arm around his shoulder. "Are you going to be alright enough to stand?”

“Yeah.”

“Are you sure?”

“Yes.” Warren was grunting as he still feels the stinging in his diaphragm.

“Are you alright?” Phoenix said, breathing heavily.

“Yeah, my..... diaphragm’s..... screwed up.” Warren grunted.

“Here, let me help you up.” Phoenix moved her hand under his armpit to pull him up from the ground. He is now standing on his feet, but still wasn’t stable enough to walk on his own. They both walked upstairs.

Phoenix took Warren in the bathroom and grabbed a washcloth and a towel from the pantry. Warren was able to stand, but was about to fall after Phoenix grabbed the washcloth.

“Warren!” Phoenix panicked. She grabbed Warren to catch his fall. She felt nervous as she holds her husband in her arms. “Are you alright?” Warren nodded to let her know he’s alright. She brought him up to his feet to keep him standing. She brought him over to the sink and turned on the cold water. "Place your arms on the sink for a minute. It'll keep you from losing your balance."

Warren put his hands on the sink as Phoenix placed the washcloth under the running water. She grabbed the green bar of soap beside the sink and rubbed it on the washcloth until it was covered with suds. "Okay, right now, what I want you to do is close your eyes and relax," Phoenix said. He closed his eyes as she gently placed the washcloth over his face to dull some of the pain and remove the blood from his nostrils. She was unbuttoning his suit jacket. "What...... are you doing?" he questioned.

"Calm down, it's alright." Phoenix unbuttoned Warren's dress shirt to reveal the damage of his diaphragm. "Oh, shit!" She panicked as there were several bruises around his ribcage and diaphragm.

"What? What's the matter?"

"Look at your chest." Warren looked down.

"Oh my God," he panicked as he saw the bruises.

"Just relax, Warren. It's only going to get worse if you panic," Phoenix said. She washed the front side of his chest. "Trust me."

Warren was feeling more stable after all of the washing. Phoenix walked behind him and took off his suit jacket and dress shirt. He was spreading both of his arms out to make it easier for her to take them off. She revealed more bruises, but there were less on his back compared to his chest.

"Oh, no, on your back, too?" Phoenix said, panicking even more. She began washing Warren's back. She grabbed the towel to dry him off. "Let's go in the bedroom. I want to talk about this." Warren looked scared, not knowing of what to do. "Don't worry, just be open. It'll be alright."

Warren and Phoenix walked into the bedroom as she turned on the light. "Go ahead, sit down on the bed," Phoenix said.

Warren sat down as Phoenix joined beside him. She looked at him and asked him some questions. "Warren, what did he do to you?" Phoenix said. He paused and looked down, thinking of what to say. He recollected himself as he looked at Phoenix.

"His name was Barrett. Barrett Atkinson, he said. He said that he has a job for me." Warren paused to think. "I told him I wasn't interested, so I refused and walked away. The next thing I know, he tackles me and starts beating the shit out of me." He was starting to shed a tear as he continued to explain. Phoenix got concerned. "I was helpless, there was only him and I. He pushed me onto a wall and continued to beat me." Tears from his eyes increased. "He kicked me to the ground and grabbed me." He was about to reach his breaking point. "He looked at me furiously and started threatening me." The pressure of the event made him wail, but continued to explain. "He mentioned you." Phoenix suddenly became startled and shocked. She started to cry right after Warren made his statement. He continued speaking, "He said if I didn't join him, he said 'It would be terrible to see something bad happened to your wife, right?'"

"Oh, Warren!" she yelled.

"He said he wants to destroy the very fabrics of society! The guy's a mad man! He doesn't give a shit about anybody and says he will stop at nothing to kill his targets." Warren placed his hand on his forehead, feeling helpless. "I'm scared, Phoenix. I don't know what to do. I don't want to lose you! I love you!"

"I love you, too," Phoenix said. They embraced and placed their chins on top of each other's shoulders to bond. Warren let his head off of her shoulders. "Phoenix, listen to me," he said. He looked into her eyes. "I promise that I will find a way to put an end to this. I gave you my word before we married that I will not let anything bad happen to you, trust me!" They started kissing.

Warren and Phoenix stood up from the bedside. They fold open the covers to prepare themselves for sleep. Warren took his clothes off until he was in his underwear. Before he climbed into bed, he walked into the hallway to turn off the light as well as the bedroom's.

Warren crawled into the folded covers as Phoenix was already laying underneath the bed sheets, covering her from the neck down. They kissed one last time before closing their eyes.

Chapter 7: Saying Goodbye

July 8, 2017

It was a warm, Saturday morning as the sun was bright. It was around nine o'clock. Warren and Phoenix were in the kitchen as the sun's rays lit up the room. There was only one light turned on, which was the ceiling light.

Phoenix was cooking breakfast on a stove. She was still wearing the same clothes from last night. The stove was silver and metallic in texture. Buttons were replaced by several touchscreen digital displays that showed the cooking temperature, the timer, and the type of cooking. She set the stove to medium as Warren could smell eggs and bacon.

Warren was wearing a white T-shirt with blue denim jeans. He was sitting by the glass doors to watch outside. Phoenix still couldn't get over what he said to her. She was still scared as her body was shaking.

Phoenix had a plate out as she scooped the eggs with the spatula and filled it onto one of them. She grabbed the tongs between the heating pads to grab pieces of bacon and set them onto the plate with scrambled eggs. "Okay, here you go," she said. She picked up Warren's plate while holding a fork and a towel under it and set it on the table.

"Thank you," Warren said.

"You're welcome, you need the energy." Warren looked down on his plate to see the thick steam come out of the food. After Phoenix walked back to the stove, she turned her head around and looked at him, giving him a smile. He wasn't paying attention until he lifted his head up. He smiled back with a chuckle. He grabbed his fork as his diaphragm was still stinging. He pierced the eggs and started eating them. After he swallowed the eggs, he sighed to relieve some stress.

"Take your time, Warren, there's no rush," Phoenix said. He pierced a strip of bacon and inserted it into his mouth.

Warren noticed a silver sedan pull into their driveway and parked behind his vehicle. He pressed his lips together as his breathing rate got faster as a black man dressed in business attire exited the vehicle. He quickly realized it was Barrett. Warren's focus turned into fear as he was walking up the porch steps with a black pistol. "Uhh.... Phoenix," he said.

"What? What's the matter?" Phoenix said. She looked into Warren's eyes in wonder.

"Get upstairs." Warren quickly got up from the chair and walked towards Phoenix.

"Why?" Phoenix was getting worried.

"Just get upstairs, please!" Warren panicked.

Barrett walked at a fast pace towards their doorstep as he kicked the glass door with brute force. He was getting enraged as he grinned his teeth while the door was starting to crack. He gave the glass door one last kick until it was nothing but cracks. He ran as he budged through it with his shoulder. As a result, the door shattered into pieces.

Barrett grunted immediately after the impact as he entered the kitchen. He looked at Warren and Phoenix angrily, dead in the eye and lifted his pistol. Warren panicked and grabbed Phoenix as they run upstairs. Barrett shot a bullet at the countertop. Phoenix was screaming in fear as Warren was taking her. As they ran upstairs side by side, Barrett just missed them by firing a bullet to the wall.

"Get in the bedroom!" Warren said, letting Phoenix go. She quickly ran into the bedroom as she sat on the bed. She covered her face with both of her hands and cried helplessly.

Warren was on the last step of the staircase. He was startled as Barrett raised his gun and pointed it to him. "Knock, knock," Barrett said arrogantly. He gave Barrett a dirty look. Barrett smirked. "So, have you made up her mind?" Barrett was walking upstairs until he was a step away from Warren.

"I told you, I'm not interested in your sick, little jobs!" Barrett got infuriated.

"Okay, then this might change your mind!" Barrett walked up to Warren and grabbed him by the shirt. He turned him around and bashed him against the staircase's wall. He turned him around again to face the bottom of the stairs and violently pushed him down. Warren's body was rolling down as he made loud thuds.

Warren's body stopped rolling as he layed helplessly on the floor of the kitchen. Barrett stomped down the stairs to approach him. As he got off the stairs, he grabbed him and repeatedly bashed him against the table. Warren was groaning in agony. His ribs were bruising as the rim of the table was impacting him. Barrett showed no remorse as he smiled and laughed, "Just like old times, huh?!"

Phoenix could hear the thudding of the table. She lifted her head and ran out of the bedroom. "Warren!" she panicked. She was running downstairs as Barrett continued to mercilessly beat her husband. She saw that Warren was coughing violently as his back was laying on the floor. She gasped.

"Warren!" she yelled, running to his aid.

"Shut up!" Barrett yelled. He turned his back and pointed his pistol at Phoenix. Her body froze in fear as the barrel of the pistol was pointed a foot from her forehead. Warren's lips pressed together to express his anger.

"If you try to intervene, I'll take you down as well," Barrett insisted. He kept the pistol pointed at Phoenix. Tears rained down from her eyes as she raised her arms.

"What do you want from us?" Phoenix said, choking up from tears. "Just tell us and we'll do it, just don't kill us!"

"Okay, this should be easy." Barrett was squeezing the trigger of the pistol.

"No!" Warren interrupted just when Barrett was about to pull the trigger on Phoenix. "Don't.... shoot." Warren coughed from the agonizing pain in his ribs. Barrett turned his head to Warren. "Hmm," Barrett said. "Finally making up your mind now, I see."

Barrett picked Warren up from the ground and pushed him onto the side of the table. Warren felt helpless and turned to Phoenix. He could see the pain in her eyes.

"Warren," Phoenix said.

"Now, join me. We have some work to do," Barrett said, pointing the gun back at Warren. He was starting to limp towards Phoenix.

"Hey, what the hell do you think you're doing?!" Barrett yelled as he was about to pull the trigger.

"No! No! Stop!" Phoenix panicked. Warren slowly turned his head to look at Barrett.

"Just... let... me... say... goodbye... to my wife at least, damn it!" Warren said in agony and anger.

Warren looked at Phoenix. Barrett lowered his gun as he gave a fierce look. Warren limped towards Phoenix to say his goodbyes.

"Phoenix, I promise...that I will never forget you," he vented.

"And I will find a way to get you out of this mess," Phoenix cried.

"You'll... always... be... in my.. heart." They hugged and

kissed.

"Enough with these charades!" Barrett interrupted. He walked up to Warren and grabbed him as soon as he let go of Phoenix. He turned Warren around as they walked around the table to exit their house.

"Warren!" Phoenix cried as she was terrified. She bent her knees to the floor and covered her face as she wailed profusely. Warren stepped on the shattered glass from the door. He grunted in pain as the glass pinched his bare feet. Barrett and Warren walked down the steps of the front porch. He pushed Warren ahead of him while they're walking on the sidewalk. Warren almost lost his balance as he flailed his arms around and was swaying left and right.

Once Barrett and Warren were on the driveway, he pushed Warren to the passenger door of Barrett's Mercedes-Benz. Barrett pulled his car keys out to feverishly unlock the door. Warren was just barely standing in front of the passenger door. Warren bent his back forward as he felt the distress of his ribs.

While Warren was opening the passenger door, Barrett quickly strides to the other side until he stopped by him. Barrett forced him into the passenger's seat. Barrett quickly pulled his seat belt down to buckle it and closed the door. He walked to the opposite side of the sedan. Warren coughed as he turned his head to see Barrett unlock the door and get in the vehicle.

Barrett buckled his seat belt and started the vehicle. "You better sit tight," Barrett said. He exited the driveway and propelled through the street.

After driving past the houses, Barrett stopped the vehicle and turned right to enter the highway. He shifted the vehicle's gears until it accelerated to sixty-five miles per hour. "What... do you want... from... me?" Warren said, worried.

"We work in numbers, Warren. I work in an organization that engages in contract killing." Warren was scared as he listened to Barrett.

"Why.. are you doing this?"

"Like I said, our organization works in numbers. Everyone

has their own unique number assigned to them. Everybody has a random code imprinted in their DNA. The number of the next person generated within the computers and advanced technology of our organization, is dead."

"You're... a... monster," Warren said as Barrett made a heartless chuckle.

"I will stop at nothing to kill the next person once their number's called! We'll discuss more of this once we get to the main building."

Warren looked straight ahead as he was scared, fearful, and helpless. Barrett kept driving on the highway to head towards the organization.

Chapter 8: Duties

July 19, 2019

"Look at me when I'm talking to you, Warren!" Barrett said. He pushed him against the wall after thinking about the events that happened. Barrett got a grip of his dress shirt and got closer in his face. "Whatever you were just daydreaming about, it's long gone now!" Warren looked at Barrett in a disgusted manner. "Give me that look all you want because you belong to us now! Nothing will change that!"

"You made me shoot a man in cold blood, what more do you want, Barrett?!"

Barrett put pressure on Warren's chest. He threatened

him, "Keep talking to me with that tone and I'll fuck you up just like I did a couple years back!" Warren just looked at Barrett. "That's what I thought." He let Warren go as he started walking beside Barrett.

Warren and Barrett stopped walking. Barrett felt something ringing and vibrating in his pocket. It was a communicator that was the shape of a circle and a silver texture. He tapped the center of its screen to open up a twelve-inch neon green holograph. "Hmm, another person being called up. That was quick," Barrett said.

The screen was generating numbers at a quick and alarming rate. After a few seconds, the numbers stopped randomizing themselves. The number came up as 723547461. A picture of a man zoomed in on the screen. The picture slid to the center as it gave basic information on the man's background. Some of the information included his name, hair color, eye color, and age.

"Darrell Friegman, Age: 26. Hair color: Black. Eye Color: Brown," Barrett said, studying the picture. Warren looked around the room as he heard that name before. "That name sounds familiar," he said quietly, but Barrett heard him.

"You know this man?"

"Not personally."

"Well, he's next. You better be ready for this." A loud alarm sounded. "Come on, we have to go!" Barrett and Warren ran to the door ahead of them and charged through it. After the door opened, they entered the dark hallway of the man they killed earlier. They budged through the double doors ahead of them and saw the clear skies. The terrain appeared to be in the middle of nowhere. There were grassy plains, hills, and hilly roads that were surrounding the parking lot. There was barb fencing enclosing the lot as the gate doors were still open. There are various types of vehicles that were parked throughout the lot of the building as they filled all of the parking spaces. They were scattered with different choices of paint colors. Most of the vehicles are composed of several luxury sedans and sports utility vehicles with the acception of a few supercars and sports cars. Barrett and

Warren's vehicles are parked right next to the entrance of the building.

Barrett climbed into the driver's seat of his Mercedes-Benz as Warren did the same. Barrett already started his vehicle and put it in reverse. He turned right and faced the gate doors.

Warren was about to buckle his seat belt. He puts the vehicle in reverse and starts to quickly follow Barrett. He saw that Barrett already turned left.

Warren propelled to eighty miles per hour to catch up beside Barrett. As they were driving away from the building, Warren could see the massively connected complex of the organization's headquarters. The numerous gray buildings were evenly spread apart in a circle. He noticed a massive line of barb fencing that could stretch out for miles.

After two days of passing, Darrell was just walking away from the automatic doors of B&N Financing as they closed behind him. The weather was sunny as the skies were clear. He waited for the roads to provide a clear space for him to cross. He saw numerous sports cars and supercars pass by as he waited.

Darrell crossed the other side of the street. He walked until he reached the entrance of the lot for Parking Garage B. He was wearing the same black shirt and blue denim jeans from the day he read the missing persons article. He typed in his WIN.

After the steel bolts disappeared into the wall, Darrell saw a Mercedes-Benz sedan pull up to where he is standing. He saw a black man open the door. It was Barrett. He walked around his front bumper until he faced Darrell on the sidewalk. "Mr. Friegman," he said. "I'd like you to come with me." Darrell became nervous.

"Who are you and what do you want?"

"Sir, I don't have time for your questions, so please don't waste my time."

"Umm, well, I have to drive home, so nice talking to you. I'm not interested, so find someone else." Darrell walked up the small steps. Barrett started to get frustrated.

"Oh, no, you're not going anywhere." Barrett went into the entrance and chased after Darrell.

As Darrell looked behind him, he saw that Barrett was sprinting after him. He quickly turned around and started sprinting at the fastest possible speed. Barrett was about ten feet away from Darrell as they ran into the parking garage.

As Barrett and Darrell entered the first floor of the building, Darrell stopped to catch his breath. He leaned up against the wall, breathing deeply. He saw Barrett running onto the steps. Darrell panicked and ran up to the second floor. Barrett was getting frustrated as he couldn't keep up with him.

Darrell stopped sprinting again to catch his breath. Barrett was still running like a cross-country runner as he entered the seventh floor. Darrell walks backwards as Barrett walked towards him. "Calm down, Darrell. I just want to talk. Don't make this harder than it has to be," Barrett insisted. He walked up to Darrell as he was still backing away. Barrett was growing impatient.

As Barrett approached Darrell, Barrett grabbed him by his shirt and lifted him off the ground. "Now, do I have to repeat myself? What's it going to be, Darrell? Are you ready to sacrifice the very foundations of what life has to offer?" Barrett raised one of his eyebrows and gave a cocky smirk.

As Barrett was about to drive his arm into Darrell's face, he caught his fist and almost bent it back, causing Barrett to let go. Barrett yelled from the pain in his wrist, which caught him off guard. Darrell's now standing on the floor.

While Barrett was distracted, Darrell clenched his fists and prepared to fight him. Darrell performed a couple blows to his diaphragm and chest. He performed an uppercut below his chin and started running up the stairs to the eighth floor. Darrell bought himself some time as Barrett was temporarily stunned from the impact. Barrett quickly recollected himself after he smeared his hand over his face. "Why, you son of a bitch!" he said in anger.

Barrett began to sprint to the stairs as he just saw Darrell run up the steps. "Yeah, you better run! I'm coming after you no matter what!" he yelled.

Once Darrell set foot on the eighth floor, he kept running until he ran down the small steps, and then across the parking floor to his yellow Volvo. There was a small amount of vehicles scattered across the floor. He quickly turned his head to see that Barrett is running down the small steps. Darrell is pressed for time as he was fumbling his hand in his pocket to find his car keys.

Darrell quickly climbed into his vehicle as Barrett was sprinting towards him. He closed the door and locked all of the other doors to prevent Barrett from getting in. He feverishly inserted the keys in the ignition to start the engine. The engine roared to life as all of the lights flashed on. He quickly puts the vehicle in reverse and backs out of the parking space. By this time, Barrett was facing him as he turned the steering wheel. Barrett raised his hands with a tempting smirk and taunts him, "Go ahead, run me over, be my guest. See if you have the guts to do it!"

Darrell jabbed the brake and put the transmission into

first gear. He floored the vehicle into drive and abruptly

turned the steering wheel to the right. He was making a quick

one hundred and eighty degree turn, facing the exit sign and

causing the tires to smoke. He almost hit Barrett with the rear

of his vehicle as he was standing a few inches away from it.

"Holy shit!" Barrett panicked.

Barrett was about to run after Darrell's vehicle again. He

floored it just in time to accelerate towards the exit. He

started sprinting after the vehicle as he was a few feet away

from him. Darrell drove on the downward ramp of the floor's

exit. Barrett was getting frustrated as it was hard to keep up

with him. After sprinting for a hundred feet, he was starting

to feel exhausted, but kept his pace. As Barrett ran down the

seventh floor, Darrell was already halfway through the exit to

quickly disappear from Barrett's sight.

After a couple minutes of passing, Darrell entered the

third floor. Barrett stopped running to catch his breath. He

pulled out his communicator and pressed the button on the

side of it, bringing up the holographic screen. There was a

wave in the center of the screen that picks up sound as a

man's voice came through. "Report," the voice said.

"I couldn't get him, he escaped," Barrett said, breathing

heavily. "Call out the reinforcements."

"Roger that, sending signals to available reinforcements."

The screen shrunk down to the center as he placed the

communicator back in his pocket.

Darrell quickly drove out of the parking garage and

through the lot. The steel bolts automatically opened as they

disappeared into the wall. Darrell turned to enter the road.

He floored the throttle as he gradually exchanged gears to

increase speed.

As Darrell continued driving, he saw a white, sharply

designed supercar turning on the road. "What the hell?" he

said in surprise. He noticed that the vehicle was turning onto

his lane in his rear-view mirror. He noticed the Pagani

emblem as the supercar accelerated closer to him with

blistering speed. "You have got to be kidding me!" he said in

panic. His heart was racing as he accelerated and switched

into third gear. He drifted to the left in a densely packed road in the city. The tires screeched aggressively, leaving marks and a small trail of smoke. He quickly regained control of his vehicle. The Pagani was still close as the driver was ten feet away from him. Darrell was constantly overtaking vehicles ahead of him.

Darrell turned and noticed the sunlight reflecting on his vehicle. The road was surrounded by buildings ranging from up to twenty stories. The Pagani still kept its pace as Darrell accelerated to eighty miles per hour. He stopped as he heard the tires loudly screech.

Darrell abruptly entered an alleyway surrounded by shadows. The Pagani continued to drive straight on the road. The buildings in between the alleyway were made of brick. He stopped in front of a green dumpster at the end of the alleyway. He saw a woman with blonde hair wearing a black shirt, denim jeans, and white tennis shoes. The woman was carrying a black pistol. He takes a closer look and noticed that it was Phoenix. Her voice sounded more mature, but still appeared young. She was pointing the gun at the windshield, "Are you one of them??!!!" Her whole body was shaking.

Phoenix walked up to the passenger door, but realized it was locked. She got frustrated and impatient, "Open the door." Darrell just looked at her in shock and disbelief. "I said open the fucking door!"

Darrell panicked and unlocked the doors. Phoenix viciously opened the door and climbed in the vehicle. She quickly lifted the pistol up to his head. "I said, are you one of them?!" she said angrily. Darrell raised his arms in panic.

"What the hell are you talking about?!"

"Are you one of the people that's responsible for kidnapping my husband?!" Darrell started to calm down as he slowly put his arms down.

"No," Darrell said. "They're after me, too." Phoenix slowly let her gun down, while still expressing some anger.

"What's going on?" Darrell questioned.

"That's what I'd like to know myself."

"Who are you?"

"Now's not the time to talk. Before I start explaining, we gotta take care of all of these bastards first." Phoenix cocked the barrel of her pistol. Darrell noticed a black Velcro belt with several ammunition clips circled around her hips.

"You drive, I'll shoot," Phoenix said, looking at Darrell seriously.

"What? Are you crazy?"

"JUST DRIVE!" Darrell taps the throttle as he drives to the side of the alleyway and exits out.

Darrell floors the throttle, causing the vehicle to jump a few inches in the air while crossing over a sidewalk. He drifts to the left. "They should be coming any minute," Phoenix said.

Phoenix looked around as there were no signs of any opposing vehicles. Darrell makes another left to face the sparkling ocean water from the other side as there was a hill of grass going downward.

Darrell looked in the rear-view mirror to see a gray Bentley coupe speeding towards him. Phoenix looked behind her to spot the vehicle. "Punch it!" she yelled. Darrell accelerated as Phoenix was readying her pistol. She leaned her head and arms out to lock her aim on the Bentley. She pulled the trigger to fire two rounds at the windshield of the British coupe.

Phoenix saw the head of a male agent come out of the vehicle with a black assault rifle in his arms. The agent was white in skin color. He has black hair while wearing sunglasses and formal attire in all black except for his dress shirt, which was white. The agent fired two three-round bursts, placing a couple bullet holes in Darrell's vehicle. Phoenix takes cover in his vehicle as he's going about ninety miles per hour. The agent now fired in a fully automatic firing mode.

The agent stopped firing at this point. Phoenix saw two more vehicles drive in between the Bentley. The vehicle on the right of the Bentley was a red high-performance sedan with the Audi emblem in the center of its grille. The vehicle to the Bentley's left was a white American muscle car with a modern appearance with the Chevrolet emblem.

"We got company!" Phoenix yelled. Darrell pushes his vehicle as he changes to fourth gear. "Your name, please," Phoenix said.

"Darrell Friegman!" he panicked as his vision blurred from the high speed.

"Darrell, I want you to do me a favor, okay?" Phoenix insisted. "When the vehicles drive beside you, ram them to the side."

"Okay." He was concentrating on the road.

The muscle car accelerated beside Darrell. He looked to see an agent aiming an assault rifle to his window. Phoenix looked at Darrell and also saw the car, "Come on, don't just sit there, ram 'em!" Darrell abruptly turned the steering wheel to impact it. He could hear the metal of the vehicles clashing together as he was ramming the vehicle. The car began to swerve after the impact. "Hit 'em again!" Phoenix yelled. Darrell rammed it a second time. It skidded out of control and hit a lamp post along with a brick building, rendering the muscle car to be severely damaged.

Phoenix peeked her head outside to take a closer look of the Audi. She heard a shotgun blast and quickly ducked under the window. She sat back up to aim at the sedan. She fired two shots at the windshield as the vehicle drove beside them. She saw that the agent already has the weapon aimed at their vehicle. "Stop!" Phoenix said to Darrell as he slammed the brake.

Darrell was driving at about thirty miles per hour. To increase the efficiency of the acceleration, Darrell lowered the transmission to first gear. "Punch it!" Phoenix said. "We're going after the red car!" Darrell floored the throttle as he switched into second gear. "When you get close, I want you to immobilize them!" Darrell accelerated to third gear as his headlights were just beside the Audi's taillight. Darrell rammed it as the vehicle spun out onto the left side of the street. The Audi's front bumper hit an entrance of a small building, damaging the vehicle significantly.

Darrell drifted to the left as the Bentley was still behind them. Phoenix quickly pulled out one of her ammunition clips and held the slide release lever of the pistol. The empty clip fell on the carpet. She inserted the new clip and prepared herself against the Bentley. Darrell kept drifting until the wheelbase straightened. He drifted to the left again, entering another road.

Darrell noticed two more vehicles with one on each side suspiciously parked in alleyways. The Bentley was still behind him. After he accelerated past the vehicles, they immediately shoot at his vehicle. The vehicles lined up between the Bentley as Darrell turned right. The vehicle by the left of the Bentley was a blue Japanese sports car by Subaru. The vehicle by the right was a black luxury sedan by Cadillac.

The three vehicles pursuing Darrell all drifted as they maintained their distance. Distracted, Darrell didn't notice the two police sedans waiting for a green light beside him. The police witnessed him and the pursuing vehicles. The police sounded their sirens and joined in the pursuit. "Oh, damn it!" Phoenix yelled.

"What's wrong?" Darrell panicked.

"Listen clearly." Darrell listened to the sirens.

"Oh, shit!" He floored the throttle. The police sedans are lined up behind the vehicles pursuing Darrell and Phoenix. The sedans had lights flashing from the centers of the doors, hood, roof, and even the rear bumper and taillights. They were produced by the manufacturer, Chevrolet. Phoenix was getting frustrated as the agents drew in closer, "I've had enough of these people!"

Phoenix peeked out of the window and shot a round at one of the Cadillac's front wheels. She heard a loud popping sound as the bullet pierced the rubber, causing the vehicle to slow down. As the Cadillac spun to the left, the agent started shooting with his assault rifle. Phoenix shot a round at the rear wheel with incredible marksmanship and accuracy. This caused the Cadillac to roll over and fly in the air just missing the police cars.

As the Subaru accelerated beside Darrell, he looked over and hesitated. He looked at Phoenix and she nodded. He looked back at the agent in the passenger seat, holding an assault rifle at him. "Hang on," Darrell said. He grunted as he turned with brute force to ram the sports car. The Subaru started spinning out of control as it reacted to the impact. All of the Subaru's tires were emanating thick layers of smoke and left skid marks across the road. It entered the grassy hill and landed into the abyss of the ocean water and sank.

Darrell straightened the vehicle. "Now, drive fast, the Bentley may put up a fight," Phoenix said. He floored the throttle as he immediately switched into fourth gear. During this time, the Volvo accelerated to just over a hundred and twenty miles per hour. He was concentrating heavily as he was overtaking the vehicles ahead of him. The driver of the Bentley didn't crack as he made the same moves as Darrell.

As the road cleared, Darrell switched to fifth gear. He reached the highest possible speed, which is just over one hundred and thirty miles per hour. The Bentley was extremely close behind Darrell's Volvo. The Bentley floored it and rammed the rear bumper. The inside of the Volvo shook violently from the impact. Darrell panicked. "Just keep driving," Phoenix said.

Phoenix turned her head and aimed at the front tire of the Bentley. The agent leaned his head out of the window with his assault rifle. As he aimed, she aimed at his arm supporting the gun. She fired one round as the bullet traveled through the agent's finger with intense velocity. He yelled in agonizing pain. The driver got distracted as he looked at his injured passenger.

Phoenix fired a round at the front wheel of the Bentley. The vehicle spun to the left as the tires leave a trail of smoke. She shot a round at the rear wheel, which caused the vehicle to spin through the air in a barrel roll, just missing the police vehicles. She was cautious, but remained calm. "Keep driving, there's no shooting the police during this. Don't want ourselves to become the NYPD's Most Wanted. That's the last thing we need right now," Phoenix said.

Darrell kept driving at full speed. "Take the next right," Phoenix said. He abruptly slowed down and drifted to the right and then to the left. The police are starting to lose their distance between them. He drifted to the right and accelerated. He was now in between buildings on both sides.

"Turn left into that alleyway and make it quick before the police spot us. We can talk from there," Phoenix said. Darrell stopped his vehicle and turned.

As Darrell entered the alleyway, he was going twenty miles per hour. They entered just in time as the police just turned on the road. The alleyway was filled with shadows as he drove between the brick buildings.

Darrell stopped in front of a dumpster and put it in park. They unbuckled their seat belts and climbed out at the same time and closed the doors. He was shocked as he saw several bullet holes around the doors and the rear bumper. The windows were all shattered except for the windshield.

Darrell and Phoenix walked up to the front bumper. They stood face to face as Phoenix folded her arms together.

"Obviously you have a lot of questions to ask," she said. Darrell couldn't believe what was happening.

"Who are you?"

"My name's Phoenix. Phoenix Leyton."

"What the hell is going on here, Phoenix?" Darrell grew desperate for answers, but composed himself.

"All of those people after you, they want you dead, and they will stop at nothing to kill you."

"But, why though? Why me?" Darrell was confused.

"Because you're the next person they want."

"But, why do they want me?" Thoughts were racing in his mind.

"The people that are after you work in an organization that eliminates people one by one as they call out their numbers."

"What do you mean by numbers?"

"Throughout the organization, they work through a system that provides a whole database of everybody's identity. Everybody in the database has their own unique number assigned to them. The system randomly generates a person's number to indicate who will be the next target. Once someone's number has been selected, the organization will do whatever it takes to take their target down." Darrell somehow understood why he's being hunted, but was scared to think about it. "And you're next in line, Darrell," Phoenix continued. "Was there a man that tried to interrogate you earlier? He drives a silver Mercedes-Benz."

"Yeah, but he couldn't keep up," Darrell said.

"His name's Barrett. Barrett Atkinson. He likes to kill for the thrill. Doesn't give a shit about anybody. He brainwashed my husband and talked him into joining the organization. His name was Warren, he was a fine man. Barrett broke into our house and started beating him," Phoenix pressed her lips together as she was getting angry, thinking about the flashbacks. "And I witnessed it. It tore me apart as he took him away from me. I have never seen him again since," Phoenix paused. "And people wonder why our society is all fucked up. It's because of shit like this."

"Sometimes I wonder about that myself," Darrell said as he looked around to recollect himself.

"We gotta get going, we need to find my husband. I've

been looking for him ever since they took him."

"What am I going to do with my car though? There are bullet holes all around it." Darrell got stressed from the vehicle's damage.

"We need to find another vehicle, we have to ditch this one. You don't usually see a vehicle with bullet holes roaming around in the city streets every day, do you?" Darrell looked at his vehicle one last time. "Nobody can know about our situation," Phoenix said seriously. "Come on, let's get out of this alleyway. Let's take a walk in the city."

Darrell and Phoenix exited the alleyway side by side. As they walked away from the vehicle, they walked on the sidewalk. They saw several pedestrians walking around. Darrell and Phoenix looked around to see the vehicles passing by within the city's infrastructure.

Chapter 9: Bad Service

July 21, 2019

Darrell and Phoenix were walking as the sun reflected its midday light. "So what do you do for a living?" Phoenix questioned.

"I work at B&N Financing, why?"

"Because we're going to need a lot of money while we're out. Do you have money with you?"

"Who doesn't?" Darrell pulled out his wallet and skimmered through the several bills he has. He saw Phoenix looking at a taxi cab coming their way. "Taxi!" she yelled.

The yellow taxi cab was slowing down until it parked

beside Darrell and Phoenix. They noticed a Ford emblem as it was a sedan. They walked to the back doors and climbed into the black leather seats and buckled their seat belts.

After Darrell and Phoenix closed the doors, they saw a man in the driver's seat wearing a black leather jacket with a white T-shirt. The dashboard was lit up with vibrant colors. It was all digital as there was a touchscreen infotainment system in the center with several touch sensitive buttons below it. Just above the system is a six inch digital display for calculating fare costs. "Where are you guys heading?" the driver said.

"Rental car service," Phoenix said. The driver entered the navigation menu. He pressed the down arrow below the ACTION button a couple times until the screen highlighted, "Voice Commands". A female computer voice spoke through the navigation system, "What will be your destination?"

"Rental car services," the driver said.

"Searching rental car services." The word, "Searching" appeared with a constantly changing ellipsis next to it. After five seconds of waiting, the driver pinpointed the nearest location on the map, which was roughly six miles away. The screen zoomed out of the three-dimensional figures representing the buildings. The taxi drove straight for about twenty yards until he turned right to follow the route of their destination.

The taxi cab stopped and turned in the parking lot of a rental car service. The building of the car service was white. The bottom half of the building had windows as Darrell and Phoenix saw the vehicles they offered. "Eighty-seven dollars, please," the driver said. Darrell pulled his wallet out and gave him a fifty and two twenty-dollar bills as the driver already had his hand open. The driver pulled open a compartment between the front seats to place the cash in there. He pulled out three one-dollar bills to give Darrell his change. "Thank you," Darrell said.

"You have a good day," Phoenix said.

Darrell and Phoenix exited the taxi cab and watched him drive off into the city as they set foot on the parking lot. "Any certain car you want?" Phoenix said while they were walking

to the entrance.

"We'll see what they have." The glass doors

automatically opened as they entered the building. The floor

was made of white linoleum tiling that was waxed as they

shined from the ceiling lights. The vehicles were sitting on top

of round wooden stands with metallic rims on the bottom of

them. There was a wide range of vehicles to choose from as

there were luxury sedans and sports cars. "Take your pick,"

Phoenix said.

As Darrell and Phoenix walked up to the counter, they

saw a salesman standing behind it with black hair while

wearing a pair of sunglasses. His skin was white as he was

wearing a black suit jacket with a white dress shirt and a black

tie. His head was tall as it almost mimicked the shape of an

upright rectangle. "Hello, how can I help you guys today?"

said the salesman.

"We're looking for a vehicle to rent for a couple days. It's

an emergency," Phoenix said.

"Alright, is there a specific reason why you guys are renting a vehicle here?" Darrell just looked at the salesman as he didn't know what to say to him. Phoenix's eyes were shifting around. "Our vehicle broke down," she said after a moment of hesitation. "But it got towed."

"So how did you guys get here?" The salesman sounded more serious.

"This was the nearest place we could find, didn't you see the taxi?" Phoenix said. The salesman raised his eyebrows in disbelief. The salesman walked away from the counter and down the small steps surrounding it. He walked to them and stood face to face. "And what kind of vehicle are you looking for today?" said the salesman in a frustrated tone.

"Something reliable," Darrell said. They walked around to look at the vehicles. They lay their eyes on a maroon BMW coupe with the rear of the vehicle facing them. The salesman noticed they were looking at it. "Is this the one you want?" the salesman said. Phoenix looked at Darrell.

"What do you think, Darrell?" he nodded his head. "We'll

take it," she said.

"That will be eighteen hundred dollars for three days."
Phoenix noticed the salesman giving her a dirty look as he
crossed his arms. "Go ahead and get frustrated with me
because I'm not in the mood today either," she said.

"Ma'am, I'm going to have to ask you to leave. You're
being very disrespectful right now-"

"Disrespectful, huh?" Phoenix got angry and walked up
to the salesman. She grabbed him by the shirt and pushed
him until he was pinned to the center of the counter. The
salesman was starting to get terrified as Phoenix got close in
his face. She pulled the pistol out of her pocket and pressed
the barrel against his cheek. "Phoenix, what the hell are you
doing?!" Darrell yelled as he was still standing beside the
BMW. Her body was shaking as she pressed her lips together.

"Do I have to repeat myself again?!" Phoenix snapped.
"I'm not in the fucking mood to play games right now! My
husband was kidnapped from God knows who and I will get
to the bottom of it! So don't waste my time, sir!" The

salesman's eyes were wide open as he was frozen in fear from the cold steel of the gun.

"Okay, ma'am! Okay! Let me get the keys for the car! Just put the gun down!" the salesman yelled.

Phoenix calmed down as she stopped shaking and slowly moved the gun away from the salesman's face. She let go of his shirt as he quickly walked up the steps to look for the car keys. The sets of keys were locked in front of small Plexiglas casings on the wall to prevent theft. "Hurry up!" Phoenix yelled. The salesman was shaking as he feverishly pulled a key out of his pocket to unlock the case holding the car keys. He pulled the handle of the casing to open it and grabbed the keys. The salesman quickly walked to the counter and set the keys on top of it. "Here, take them, use it as long as you want. Car's yours!" he said nervously. Phoenix walked up to grab the keys.

"Good, because I'm never renting a vehicle from this place again!" Phoenix walked to the front passenger door of the BMW. "Let's go, Darrell." She threw the keys to him as he caught them with his hands. He walked to the vehicle and unlocked it. He pressed a button on the door panel to unlock the passenger door.

Darrell and Phoenix climbed into the vehicle as they saw the stitched, black leather seats. They looked at the dashboard to notice the advanced technologies.

The interior appeared fresh as it looked like it just came out of the factory. There was an infotainment system in the middle as the several gauges behind the steering wheel were all digital except for the fuel gauge. Just below the infotainment system were vents for the temperature settings followed by an AM/FM radio below it. There was an airbag that was sitting just above the center console. The rim of the console was silver as there were several buttons.

Darrell started the vehicle. The lighting of the interior was a bright shade of red on the several gauges behind the steering wheel.

Darrell put it in reverse and turned right to face the glass entrance doors. The salesman started to feel uneasy. "Drive,"

Phoenix said. He set the transmission into drive as he propelled to the doors. The salesman panicked as he ran down the steps to sprint towards the vehicle, "No, no, no! Not the doors!" The doors started to open as the vehicle accelerated closer. The doors shattered to pieces as it drove through and entered the parking lot. "Holy shit!" the salesman said as he ran to the shattered glass.

Darrell stopped to wait for other vehicles to pass. No vehicles were close as they were a few blocks away. He abruptly turned right. Phoenix leaned towards Darrell to check the fuel gauge. "Perfect, we have a full tank. We're going to need as much as we can in case they decide to come back," Phoenix said. Darrell turned left as Phoenix took out the clip to check the leftover ammunition in the pistol. Phoenix pulled some bullets out of her ammunition pouch and began loading the clip until it was full. "And plenty of firepower, too," she continued. She inserted the magazine back in the gun and cocked the barrel.

Chapter 10: Sacrifice

As Darrell turned, sounds of car engines came from behind. Phoenix widened her eyes and leaned her head out of the window to look behind. She saw three vehicles accelerating towards their way. She got back in the car to warn Darrell, "We have company, punch the gas!"

Darrell looked in the rear view window. He floors the throttle as he turns onto another lane to overtake the vehicle in front of him. The engine roared as he drifted to the left to see the ocean waters.

As Darrell straightened his vehicle, he saw two silver

sedans turning left from in between buildings and drove in the oncoming lanes beside him. The three vehicles behind him were about to turn as they are twenty feet away.

The sedans accelerated to catch up with Darrell. "Phoenix, there's more!" he yelled. Phoenix looked to see the sedans. She realized that it was Barrett and aimed it at the window beside Darrell. "Hold still, Darrell," Phoenix said.

Phoenix looked to see the other person driving beside Barrett. She was in shock and gasped, slowly letting her gun down. "Warren," she said in disbelief. Warren was wearing a pair of sunglasses with the same attire as Barrett. "We gotta take these guys down behind us quick!" Phoenix panicked.

"What's wrong?!" Darrell panicked.

"Look to your left." Darrell looked at the sedans. "Warren's beside Barrett."

The three vehicles fired at the rear with their assault rifles. Darrell was getting nervous, but maintained his concentration. Phoenix shifted her eyes and aimed her pistol at the opposing vehicles.

The three vehicles were lined up beside each other as they were all different colors. The vehicle in the middle was a white American luxury Lincoln sedan. To the right of the Lincoln was a red Italian luxury high-performance Maserati coupe. To the left was a black American luxury high-performance Cadillac sedan.

The agent in the Maserati started shooting at Darrell's vehicle. Phoenix slipped her head back in to take cover. She fired two rounds at the front bumper as the bullets traveled at split-second velocity. She took cover again as the agent resumed firing.

As Darrell was overtaking two vehicles, he looked in his side mirror and saw two black armored sports utility vehicles turn to where Warren and Barrett are driving. The armored vehicles kept accelerating until they were right behind them. "Oh shit!" Darrell panicked.

"What's the matter?" Phoenix yelled. She looked into the back seats and noticed the vehicles. She immediately turned her head back and prepared her pistol. "Keep driving, keep switching gears if you have to!" Phoenix yelled.

Darrell switched to third gear. His and Phoenix's bodies felt lighter as the BMW accelerated at an alarming rate. He was gaining distance from the three vehicles behind him. Barrett and Warren accelerated, quickly regaining distance with Darrell and Phoenix.

Darrell saw Barrett rolling down his passenger window. He was holding a pistol and pointed it at him. He fired a round at Darrell's vehicle. Phoenix noticed the armored vehicles were coming closer to Barrett and Warren. She was getting angry as the armored vehicles entered the road that Darrell's on.

The armored vehicles moved up in front of the pursuing vehicles. Phoenix leaned her head out and saw the armored vehicles containing thick plating, bearing the Porsche emblem. "Oh, these people are really pissing me off!" she said in anger before slipping back in the vehicle.

Darrell accelerated into fourth gear. The armored vehicles slowly caught up as Darrell and Phoenix heard the boisterous roars of the V8 engines behind them. One of the armored vehicles bumped the rear of the BMW.

The armored vehicles accelerated until they matched Darrell's distance. They started driving beside them. Phoenix aimed her pistol at the vehicle to her right, but quickly realized she couldn't shoot at the window. The windows were made of bulletproof glass. She shifted her eyes around the vehicle to find a weak spot. She looked down the rapidly spinning chrome alloys. The type of tires matched to regular commuting drivers.

Phoenix regained her focus as she aimed the pistol at the front tire. Before the armored vehicle turned to ram the BMW, she fired a round just in time to hear it pop. The tire was spinning on its rim as it created a shower of sparks. "Now ram 'em!" she said to Darrell.

Phoenix slipped her head in right before Darrell forcefully rammed the vehicle. The armored vehicle started to swerve. "Hit 'em again!" she yelled. Darrell rammed the vehicle again. He was getting frustrated, "Why aren't they budging?!"

After ramming the armored vehicle one more time, it swerved onto the grass. The vehicle flew in the air while driving up a surfaced part of the grass. It came to a stop as it hit a brick building, with its roof impacting first. The damage involved shattered windows ranging from the windshield to the back seats. "Damn!" Darrell yelled, reacting to the damage. The armored vehicle fell onto the grass with its front bumper touching the ground. The right side of the BMW is slightly dented from the ramming. "The tires are their weak spot! I'll shoot the tires, and you ram them! When you hear the pop of the tire, that's your signal!" Phoenix said.

"Got it!" Darrell said.

"Now keep driving, only switch lanes to overtake the vehicles, open the sunroof!" Phoenix unbuckled her seat belt and climbed into the back seats. Darrell pressed a button in the center console to open the sunroof. The sun gave light as she climbed up with her head and chest touching the roof. She pressed her body up against the roof to keep her balance.

She grasped the pistol with both of her arms and aimed it at

Barrett's sedan.

Before Phoenix was about to fire a round at one of

Barrett's tires, the armored vehicle from behind them

rammed the rear. She panicked as she almost lost her grip on

the roof. She quickly pulled herself back in the BMW before

the armored vehicle rammed again. She got back in the

passenger seat beside Darrell and buckled it back up.

The armored vehicle turned left and accelerated until it

was beside Darrell. He rammed the armored vehicle a couple

times before it swerved. It lost enough control to crash into

the Cadillac. The Cadillac's front bumper impacted the rear of

the armored vehicle with brute force, rendering it useless.

Phoenix went back to the sunroof and shot a round at

the front tires of the Maserati, which created showers of

sparks as they were spinning on its rims. After driving mainly

on its rims, the vehicle swerved. The vehicle began to

perform barrel rolls, damaging many areas of the vehicle. The

front bumper including the hood was severely damaged from

impact as the windshield and front windows were shattered.

Phoenix puts her focus on the flawless Lincoln. She aimed at the front tires as it accelerated to the rear bumper of the BMW. She fired two rounds as the tires popped. Once the Lincoln swerved, she saw its back tires leave a trail of smoke and screeched. Darrell was losing distance with the Lincoln. She fired a bullet into the rear tire of its wheelbase.

The Lincoln flew in the air while performing a series of barrel rolls. The barrel rolls came to a close as its roof flattened by impacting a brick building. The car windows shattered on impact as the roof was severely dented.

There was only Barrett and Warren left. Phoenix only has a few bullets left in her clip. She turned her attention to Barrett.

Phoenix unbuckled her seat belt and climbed up the sunroof. She stretched her arms out and locked her aim onto Barrett. "You're finished, Barrett," she said to herself. Barrett gave her a devious smirk.

As Phoenix was about to pull the trigger, Barrett turned

his head to face Warren. He quickly turned left and heartlessly rammed Warren. His vehicle started to screech as it swerved to the left, causing the vehicle to be severely damaged.

Warren was spinning out of control. He started to panic as he was constantly spinning the steering wheel in both directions. He was getting dizzy as his vision was blurring from the world around him. His vehicle started to tip over as it entered a series of barrel rolls.

Phoenix gasped as she couldn't believe her eyes. "WARREN!" she yelled in shock. Barrett turned left to enter the interior of the city. Phoenix feverishly pulled herself back inside. "Stop the vehicle and turn around!" she panicked. Darrell violently thrusts the brake as he heard the loud screeching of the tires and makes a U-turn to the other side. He quickly shifted back down to first gear to increase acceleration efficiency. He floored it and felt the hard acceleration as he drove to Warren's battered vehicle.

While driving towards the crash scene, Darrell thrusts

the brake. He came to a stop just a few feet away from it. The Mercedes-Benz was completely totaled. The vehicle was sitting on its wheelbase as there were huge dents and paint scrapes all around it. All of the car windows were shattered from the impact.

Warren slowly opened the door and collapsed to the ground. He was grunting and coughing from the pain in his severely damaged body. He also has a bloody nose. He could barely move from the pain coursing through him.

Darrell and Phoenix opened their doors and ran to Warren. "Warren!" Phoenix panicked. Once she was standing beside Warren's body, she crouched down to place her arm under his back. Darrell came up to his body and crouched down in front of his feet. "Are you okay?" Phoenix said as she brushed his hair.

Warren said as he was trying to speak, "I........ can't....... move." Phoenix was getting worried.

"We have to get you to a hospital. I'll call 911-"

"No," Warren interrupted.

"No? But why, Warren? Look at the shape you're in, you're battered up all around your body."

"I'm...... afraid...... I..... can't...... come..... with.... you." Phoenix was surprised from what came out of Warren. Her emotions escalated as tears came down, "But, Warren, we can help you. We can get you out of this mess." His speech was becoming more delayed, "He....... made......... me...... shoot....... someone........ in.......... cold........ blood. Even....... if.... you..... try..... to.... help.... me........ now......., they'll...... immediately...... come... after.... you......, no..... matter... who.... helps... me."

"Warren, please, trust me, I want to help you, we can start over." Warren was growing weaker from the pain, "Phoenix........., listen....... to......... me........ and....... you........... listen....... good. The............. number...... of...... people.......... within......... the.. organization......... are....... growing..................... stronger........... after........ every........ person............ they kill."

"What are they going to do, Warren?"

"They're................. building......... an......... army..........
to........ take........... down............ every............. last................
person................ that....... is....... their....... next........ target."
The tears in Phoenix's eyes increased as Warren grew weaker.

Phoenix cried, "Please, Warren, stay with me, it'll be okay."

"Phoenix..............., I....................... want..................
you............... two............. to............. take........... that...........
son...... of...... a....... bitch......... down........ and........ shut......
down......... the........... system........... before.............
it's........... too........... late."

"Warren, please don't go, I'll find you a way out of this mess, just hang in there," Phoenix begged as she was about to reach her breaking point.

"I'm....................... not.......................
doing.................... this.................. for................
me................., I'm........................ doing........................
this.................... to...................... protect................
you................... and............. the............. people.............

that.............. walk.............. on.................. the.................

very................... features................. of...............

our... planet," Warren

concluded as he slowly closed eyes.

"Oh, Warren," Phoenix said. She was wailing as she layed

her head down on his chest.

Phoenix lifted her head up as she didn't feel Warren's

chest rise. "Warren?" Phoenix said. "WARREN?" No response.

She realized he was dead. "NOOOOOOOOOOO!" She yelled in

melancholy and agony as she mourned down on him. Darrell

was beginning to shed a tear.

"Phoenix, we have to go," Darrell said. He stood on his

feet. He walked around Warren's body to crouch down beside

Phoenix, "Come on, we have to go, Phoenix. I know it's hard,

but we can't stay. It's not safe here." He stood back up and

grabbed Phoenix. He walked backwards and pulled her

towards the BMW.

"NO! NO! Let me go!" Phoenix was trying to pull herself

free from Darrell's grip.

"Come on, Phoenix!" Darrell kept pulling her until he opened the passenger door. He picked her up and set her on the passenger seat and closed the door. He walked around the coupe to open the driver's door. Around the BMW were several dents and paint scrapes on both sides as well as some bullet holes.

Darrell noticed that Phoenix was looking over Warren's body. She had her arms crossed as she was still crying. Darrell came inside and started the vehicle. "Warren," Phoenix gloomily said to herself. Darrell accelerated to forty-five miles per hour. "I made that promise two years ago," Phoenix said. "I promised to him that I will find a way to put an end to this," she paused. "And I will make sure that motherfucker pays and burns in hell along with it!"

Phoenix pulled out her gun and let the clip fall on her hand. She grabs eight bullets from her pouch. She inserted the bullets into the clip one by one. She pushed the clip back in the gun and cocked the barrel to prepare herself for the events ahead of them.

Chapter 11: Looking Back

As the day turned to night, Darrell and Phoenix were sitting on a bench on a grassy ledge as they distantly looked over the Brooklyn Bridge. The lights of the buildings glowed behind it. The obsidian skies showed no clouds as they saw the light of the waning moon shine down on the ocean's waters. The sky projected an irregular pattern of stars. "You know, I've always wondered about this city," Phoenix said and looked at Darrell. She talked in a delusional, yet calm tone of voice, "So mysterious, yet so beautiful on the inside, the thought of it just messes with your mind."

"It's always been like this in New York City," Darrell said.

Phoenix looked away from Darrell to think about something.

"Do you want to know something about Warren?" Phoenix

asked. He didn't say anything, but she knew he was paying

attention. She sighed. "Warren's life wasn't the best even

from the start," she started off. "Barrett reminded him of his

childhood." She paused. "It all started in his teenage years.

Warren's father, Johnathon Leyton, was never there for him.

His father worked in an organized crime syndicate for several

years until authorities decided to charge him for seventeen

counts of murder and lock his ass up in prison. He was abused

by his father. His parents didn't give a shit about him."

Phoenix paused as she felt like crying. "Warren tried to talk

his father out of the things he was doing, but that didn't

work. His father grabbed him and threw him onto the bedside

of his room. His father started beating him until he stared

Warren down and looked at him right in the face. His father

didn't say anything to him after that. Warren layed on the

floor crying not just from the physical pain, but was broken by the heartlessness from his father." Darrell looked down as he was visualizing the event. "Johnathon abused his mother as well, but she wasn't the best either. All she cared about was her *damn* money. She was always getting into trouble with the law. She had a habit of stealing vehicles. She didn't care what the vehicle was whether it was old or new, just as long as it involved money. She was never concerned for Warren. All she cared about was herself."

Phoenix talks about the day she met him, "Warren and I both met on my first day of work at B&N Financing. He was a fine man, indeed. He noticed that I was missing an important piece of my paperwork and handed it to me. I was grateful." Phoenix laughed to herself. "Later that day, we decided to sit down together during lunch hour. One thing that I really admired about him was his openness. Once he explained to me about his childhood, I was already a listener. We decided to get married in 2014 after two years of dating. About three years later when Warren was working the night shift, I got a call from him telling me that someone named Barrett

Atkinson beat him up. He was lucky to survive that day, because his diaphragm was all screwed up. It wasn't long until Warren walked to our doorstep. As I slid open the door, he was feeling weak. He wasn't strong enough to stand on his feet. He explained to me what happened earlier that night. That's when the trouble started with Barrett."

Phoenix teared up, "I was scared for him. I obviously didn't know what to do. I couldn't stop thinking about the scenario. The next day, I was feeding him breakfast, just trying to get through the day. That's when Barrett decided to come to our house. Warren told me to go upstairs to hide in the bedroom. As I was up there, I heard Barrett maliciously beating him against the kitchen table. Warren was screaming in agony. I ran down the stairs to see if he was okay, but he was feeling weak once again. Warren couldn't leave before saying goodbye though. After he made his goodbyes, Barrett pulled him out of my sight and took him out of our house. I never saw him again since." Phoenix paused as tears flood down her eyes, "After that all happened, I was never able to see or think straight ever again."

Phoenix bent her back and placed her hands over her face as she was touching her knees. "I just wish I could turn back and save him," Phoenix said, feeling regret.

Darrell slid over beside Phoenix to give her a hug as she set her head on Darrell's shoulder. "Please help me, Darrell," Phoenix begged. She closed her eyes as Darrell slowly rubbed his hand around her back. He was about to speak, "The way our society is, the whole system works in mysterious ways. Some people don't see it coming, which is what pisses me off about some people. Hell, some people are even so heartless that when there's a horrible crime being committed while they're witnessing it up close, they don't give a shit enough to even report it. That's one of the things that I hate about the society we live in today."

Darrell looked at Phoenix, "Phoenix, look at me." Phoenix opened her eyes and faced Darrell. "I want you to listen to me and I want you to listen good, alright?" Darrell said firmly. "That man out there, he's up to something. As long as we sit around, he's going to continue to find ways to kill the next target. If we stay here, he will continue to send reinforcements after us and we won't stand a chance."

Phoenix was still crying as he saw small blood vessels around her eyes.

Darrell puts his arms on Phoenix's shoulders, "Phoenix, we have to stop Barrett. You said to your husband that you would find a way to end this, right?" Phoenix nodded her head. "We have to get going, do this for your husband. He needs to rest in peace." Darrell let go of her shoulders as they stood up from the bench. "Come on."

Darrell and Phoenix walked from the ledge and back to their vehicle. It was parked by a lamp post and a sidewalk. The BMW was sitting beside brick buildings that appeared historical in texture. It was sitting next to a turn on the outskirts of New York City.

Darrell unlocked the door as Phoenix was behind him. They both climbed into the vehicle. The engine roared as the headlights immediately flashed on. He put the vehicle into drive and turned right into the dim roads.

Darrell accelerated to thirty miles per hour. "We're going to have to get out of the city by tomorrow," he said. "Barrett and the rest of his organization will be stepping up their game at any moment," he continued. "We're going to have to be prepared for what's ahead at all costs."

"Don't worry, I have plenty of preparation at my disposal," Phoenix said boldly. Her pouch on her Velcro belt was almost three-quarters full. "Let's finish this," Phoenix said earnestly.

"That's what I like to hear," Darrell said.

After a half of a mile of driving, Darrell stopped and turned right to go through a vast series of turns for exiting downtown. As Darrell makes every turn, they eventually head into the deep valleys of the dark outskirts of New York City.

Chapter 12: The Final Hour

July 22, 2019

The next morning, Darrell and Phoenix were driving on straight roads surrounded by grassy plains with a couple wind turbines in the distance. The skies were as clear as there were no clouds. There were transformers and power lines that extended for miles. The BMW was operating at eighty miles per hour as there were no signs of vehicles. There are four lanes on both sides. "Do you see anything, Phoenix?" Darrell said. She glanced at her side mirror, but nobody was behind them.

"Right now, we're clear, keep driving though, these

power lines must lead to somewhere," Phoenix said. He slightly pressed on the throttle.

Darrell heard a small and quiet noise behind him. He glanced at his side mirror. "Shit!" he yelled in panic. He floored the throttle and switched to third gear. Phoenix's body was pulling back from the sudden jolt of acceleration.

"Whoa, Darrell, easy! What's the matter?" Phoenix said, becoming alert.

"We've got visitors!" Phoenix looked in her side mirror. She noticed three vehicles coming their way as they accelerated at blistering speeds. "Shit! They must've known we were coming this way!" Phoenix said. As the vehicles got louder, she noticed that they're sharper and stylish in appearance, "They're driving supercars! Darrell, go as fast as you can right now!"

The vehicles pursuing the BMW are lined up side by side. The vehicle in the middle was a cream white Aston Martin coupe. The vehicle to the Aston Martin's right was a neon green Italian Lamborghini supercar. The vehicle to the left was a sky blue Ford muscle car with a modern appearance. The Ford has a major performance package as it matched the other vehicles driving beside it.

Darrell smacked the throttle as the hard acceleration propelled the BMW. The driver of the Aston Martin floored it until its front bumper came in contact with the BMW. Darrell and Phoenix yelled in panic as the interior shook violently. Phoenix said, "We must be close to their base! We gotta take care of these guys behind us! That must explain the types of vehicles they're driving! These could be the more elite agents we're facing up against!"

The Lamborghini accelerated beside Darrell as he heard the whistling V12 sound. He looked in his side mirror to notice a few more vehicles coming in the distance. He noticed two black armored SUVs in front of three supercars that are red, white, and orange in color. His vision and focus blurred as he continued to accelerate.

Phoenix turned her head to face the Lamborghini. The driver rolled down the window as she saw the passenger loading the magazine of an assault rifle. The driver had a

black shade of sunglasses as he was white in skin color. The

passenger handed the assault rifle to the driver. The driver

lifted his arm carrying the assault rifle as he pressed it against

his shoulder. He is now driving with only one arm on the

steering wheel.

Phoenix paused with an expression frozen with fear. "Any

last words?" said the driver. He moved the barrel closer to her

forehead. "Phoenix, there's more!" Darrell yelled. Her body

started to shake as she felt desperate for a solution. She

looked over to see the armored vehicles and supercars.

Phoenix turned her head back to face the driver. The

driver gave a smirk while raising one of his eyebrows. He was

slowly pulling the trigger. Her fear turned into focus as she

looked at the gun. Without warning, her focus turned to

anger as she quickly pushed the rifle to her left and grabbed

the center of the gun. The driver was stupefied as she was

forcefully turning the gun around. They started pulling the

gun back and forth while grinning their teeth. The driver was getting frustrated, but Phoenix maintained her control.

After Phoenix performed one more invigorating pull, she finally grabbed a hold of the assault rifle. The driver panicked as his arm was free from the gun. She's holding the rifle with both of her arms. She started to bash the driver's head with the butt of the rifle.

After the driver took a couple bashes to the head, Phoenix turned the gun around. "Thanks for the gun!" Phoenix said angrily. She fired at the driver as the bullets exited out with intense velocity. The driver's body was shaking as the bullets pierced through him.

The Lamborghini was starting to lose control. As the vehicle was swerving, the armored vehicle behind it rammed the vehicle from the rear. The wheelbase of the supercar was leaving a thick trail of smoke. The spinning of the supercar increased in revolutions as it spun off of the road and came to a stop.

Phoenix leaned over the window. She was locking her aim on the Aston Martin and started shooting at the vehicle.

After shooting ten rounds, a couple bullet holes were visible on the windshield and the hood of the car. The vehicle was still going strong as it kept its distance with the BMW. "Drive faster!" Phoenix yelled at Darrell.

Darrell punched the throttle to higher revs in the third gear. He then switched into fourth gear. The growling roar of the BMW grew louder as he accelerated. "That's what I like to hear!" Phoenix said.

Phoenix noticed the passenger window of the Aston Martin roll down as an agent leaned out with an assault rifle. He drew his gun and aimed it at Phoenix as he pressed the butt of the gun against his collar bone. The agent was about to pull the trigger. Phoenix shot a burst of three rounds just in time before he fired his weapon. The agent's arms are stunned as he screamed in excruciating pain from the bullets that entered his shoulder. The driver is startled as he looked upon his injured passenger.

While the driver was distracted, Phoenix aimed at the driver and fired at the windshield. As the bullets pierced through, the driver started jumping in the seat after every bullet entering his body. The bullets rendered the driver dead as he made no movement.

As the Aston Martin began to slow down, it approached the front bumpers of the armored vehicles. The armored vehicle from the left side of the BMW began to accelerate. They were both made from Porsche. The armored vehicle beside of the Aston Martin abruptly turned right to push it out of its way. The vehicle screeched as it spun off into the grassy plains.

The armored vehicle turned right until it was beside the BMW's shattered taillights as Darrell heard the blasting tumult of the engine. Phoenix locked her aim on the front wheels of the vehicle. She fired a three round burst, causing it to pop. "You know the drill!" Phoenix yelled. She slipped back in the vehicle just in time before Darrell repeatedly rammed the vehicle. After several impacts, the armored vehicle swerved multiple times as it entered the grassy plains.

The second armored vehicle behind them accelerated to

the BMW's right side. Phoenix slipped back out and locked

her aim at the vehicle's front wheelbase. She fired at both of

the tires, causing them to pop and the rims to make showers

of sparks. The vehicle kept going, but was losing speed.

The red supercar behind the armored vehicle noticed its

rear coming closer to it. The car slammed on the brake, but

was going too fast to react. The driver of the armored vehicle

looked up at his rear view mirror to notice the Ferrari

emblem fast approaching. The Ferrari impacted the vehicle

with extreme force, causing it to be damaged beyond repair.

The hood and front bumper drastically changed shape as the

windshield was also affected during the impact. Phoenix

slipped back in the vehicle after she heartlessly witnessed the

crash.

The blue Ford was accelerating beside Darrell. As the

Ford's passenger window rolled down, an agent pulled out

yet another assault rifle. Darrell noticed he was checking his

weapon. He abruptly turned left to ram the muscle car with a

flawless attempt. The wheelbase of the Ford swerved to the

left, following a series of barrel rolls onto the oncoming side. The overall damage rendered the vehicle useless after it landed on its wheelbase.

There were only two vehicles left, the white and orange supercars. Darrell looked in the rear view mirror to see them increasing speed as they accelerated closer. Darrell was getting angry. "I'm just getting started!" he said brazenly. He switched into fifth gear and propelled to a hundred and sixty miles per hour, almost reaching top speed. The excessive amounts of adrenaline were coursing through his body as he accelerated.

The supercars were twenty feet away from the BMW. The orange supercar is beside Darrell's left as he noticed a McLaren emblem and had a modern appearance.

Darrell looked in the rear view mirror again to see the white supercar. "That's the same Pagani that played chicken with me yesterday!" he said. The driver of the McLaren abruptly turned right to ram the BMW. The vehicle slid while reacting from the impact. Darrell panicked, but quickly regained focus as he straightened it out. He abruptly turned left to ram the McLaren, but the vehicle barely budged at all. The McLaren rammed again as the metal of both vehicles were grinding against each other, creating small showers of sparks.

As Darrell was being pushed into the last of four lanes, his wheelbase straightened just in time before he touched the grass. He saw his chance, so he turned to push the McLaren to the far side of the road. The car's passenger window formed cracks as he continued to callously ram the vehicle along with several dents and paint scrapes. He rammed the vehicle one more time with belligerent force. The McLaren started to tip over and perform several barrel rolls until it came to a stop in the middle of the oncoming lanes.

Darrell straightened his vehicle until it was lined up with the white supercar. He turned right onto another lane. Phoenix was getting worried as he tapped on the brake, "Darrell, what are you doing?" The BMW was falling back until he was beside the Pagani. "Hang on," he said. He abruptly turned left to ram the vehicle. The driver of the vehicle turned to the opposite of Darrell. Both vehicles are grinding against each other. Darrell was grunting as the Pagani was pushing him closer to the grass.

Just before Darrell was about to touch the grass, he regained control as the Pagani stopped turning. Darrell grunted as he turned to push the Pagani to the oncoming lanes. The driver attempted to push Darrell again into the grass. This time, he is pushed by only one lane. Darrell turned again to forcefully push the Pagani near the oncoming lanes.

As the Pagani was about to ram Darrell, he delivered a devastating impact without warning. The car violently swerved and performed a series of barrel rolls as it flew a few feet in the air. The Pagani landed as it rested on the oncoming lanes, rendering the vehicle useless.

Darrell straightened the vehicle. "Are you crazy, Darrell?!" Phoenix said.

"Yes, I am." He continued to follow the power lines. He

approached a slowly descending hilly road. He noticed several

buildings within the distance as he noticed the raised grassy

plains between them. "Whoa," they said in awe.

Darrell and Phoenix started to see more buildings as they

were all connected into one massive complex. They realized

they were entering in the middle of nowhere as there were

no other facilitations to house civilization. "I think we found

where they were coming from," Darrell said. He entered onto

a straight and smooth road as he exited the descending hill.

Phoenix looked anxiously around the complex. She was

getting frustrated, "There's got to a be a way in." Phoenix

panicked as she looked for an entrance. She spotted a gray

building with a half empty parking lot of vehicles. She saw a

pair of silver double doors on the building. Phoenix said,

"We'll try going in there, that could be a way in." She pointed

at the double doors, catching Darrell's attention. "Pull into

the parking lot."

Darrell abruptly stopped as him and Phoenix leaned

forward from the deceleration. Once they stopped beside the

parking lot, he turned right to find a parking space in the far

side of the lot. "Park into there," she said. Darrell parked next

to a sedan.

Darrell and Phoenix unbuckled their seat belts as he

feverishly pulled the keys out of the ignition. They quickly

opened the doors and got out. Phoenix leaves her assault rifle

behind on the passenger seat and only carries her pistol. They

closed the doors and sprint to the double doors. They moved

in different directions as they ran through the empty parking

spaces. They started to hyperventilate while running.

As Darrell and Phoenix exited the lot, they ran up the

small steps towards the doors. Phoenix had false hope as she

noticed a touchpad with numbers that was similar to a layout

of a telephone. "Shit!" she said as she frustratingly hit the

door with her palm.

"How are we supposed to get in?" Darrell said angrily.

"Simple!" Phoenix aimed at the touchpad and fired two

rounds, causing it to short out. Darrell was in shock of what

just happened. "What? You told me to be prepared," Phoenix

said. She raised her eyebrow and spun the gun around with her finger.

Darrell and Phoenix ran into the doors and entered the dimly lit hallway. They sprinted to the doors ahead of them. While a couple feet away, they charged at the doors to open them. They looked around to see three brightly lit hallways around them. They see a set of double doors on both sides of the hallway. They looked straight to see a hallway that extends to a few hundred feet.

As Phoenix looked to the right, she noticed a gray door next to the white double doors off to the side. "There must be a way in there," she said. "You take the side, I'll take the double doors." They sprinted towards their doors.

As Darrell was about to push open his door, Phoenix wanted to think of a plan. She had to stop him. "Shhhhhhhh!" She pointed her finger to her lips. She walked up to Darrell and whispered to him, "We don't know what's behind these doors. We can't risk another life being taken. We have to be quiet and fast if we both want to make it out of this place alive." Darrell looked at her in a serious manner. "We can do this, Darrell, trust me." He shifted his eyes to the floor and looked back up to Phoenix. He slowly nodded his head. "We have to get going," she said. "That bastard's probably in there." They slowly opened the doors.

As the door closed behind Darrell, the hallway he walked in was pitch black. He walked straight to see a dim ray of light ahead of him from the side. As he walked closer, he saw Barrett standing in front of several television monitors. He had both of his hands behind his back.

Darrell exited the hallway to enter into a small control room. He walked to the center of the aisle of the metallic floor. "It's over, Barrett," he said. Barrett turned around to face him. "Darrell, so nice of you to join me," Barrett said as he removed his hands from his back. He slowly walked to Darrell as he looked around with a cunning smile. "Take a look around you, Darrell. All of this fancy work that the agents put in this organization, I couldn't ask for anything better than this." Darrell got angry as Barrett was walking to him.

"Don't you realize what you're doing? You've killed countless numbers of unsuspecting, yet innocent people that walk on this planet!" Barrett showed no remorse. "And Warren, he wasn't even a number, but you killed him anyway! You brainwashed him into doing your bidding! He didn't deserve any of this! You pretty much put him through hell over nothing!"

"Yeah, but he needed to go, anyways. I never liked the man to begin with. I hated his guts. The organization needed a new recruit. So I chose him, which made him an easy target. He had that one thing I always wanted, which was money. He was a wealthy man, indeed." Darrell was infuriated. "You know why I took his life, Darrell? It's because he was never fit from the start. He was abused when he was younger. He let everything get to him. Failure was the only thing he knew."

"No, it's because you're a coward. He never had a chance in life because of you!"

Barrett snapped and charged at Darrell. He tackled Darrell to the ground and clenched his fists to punch him.

Darrell grabbed Barrett's fist and twisted it around. He gave in as he grunted from the twist, so Darrell punched Barrett in the middle of his chest. The punch caused him to get off of Darrell as he stood up from the ground.

Darrell was about to throw a couple more punches. Barrett crossed his arms in an X over his upper body to defend himself before Darrell could do his damage. He uncrossed his arms and forcefully wrapped himself around Darrell's diaphragm and back and threw him onto the ground. The front of Darrell's body was facing the floor. Barrett grabbed the back of his head and pressed it down against the ground. He was enraged, "Now, this is only going to take a moment, Darrell. DON'T waste my time as I put you to sleep, permanently!"

Phoenix was hiding behind a dark wall as there was a platform a few feet ahead of her. She aimed at the floor with both of her hands. Barrett started driving his fist into Darrell's chest. He grunted from the hard knuckles of his punches. "Now, Darrell, do you have any last words?" Barrett said.

Phoenix slowly walked to the platform. As she was by the edge, she locked her aim on Barrett's shoulder. She pulled the cold steel of the trigger and fires a round. The bullet whistled while traveling through Barrett's body. He screamed in agonizing pain as the blood gushed from his shoulder. He looked up at the platform to see Phoenix aiming at him, "Im...... possible!" Barrett yelled in anguish.

"Just face it, Barrett. Your number's up!" Phoenix aimed at his forehead and fired another bullet. His head flew back as the bullet traveled through his skull. His body was frozen for a brief moment and then collapsed on the metallic floor. The blood from his forehead leaked as he was laying on the floor motionless.

Darrell was free from Barrett's grip as he moved his body away from him and stood on his feet. He was groaning from the pain in his chest. "You alright, Darrell?" Phoenix yelled.

"Ribs.... hurt, but... I'm good."

"Let's get out of here." Darrell slowly walked into the hallway and opened the door. Phoenix ran away from the platform and ran down the steps to open the double doors.

Chapter 13: For Warren

Darrell and Phoenix met each other in the hallway and walked beside each other. They walked towards the center of the three hallways. Darrell was grunting from the pain. "You sound really bad, are you okay?" Phoenix said.

"Yeah...., I'm.... fine," Darrell replied.

"Let me see your chest." They stopped walking. Phoenix gently lifted up his shirt. "Oh, God, Darrell," she panicked. There were a couple swelled bruises on the bottom of his chest.

"We have to get you to a hospital-"

"Phoenix...., it's... okay. They're.. bruises... he.. didn't.. brake... any.. bones." Phoenix hesitated and looked at Darrell. She pulled his shirt back down. They resumed walking and turned left to enter the entrance hallway. They walked to the double doors to see the clear skies from outside. They walked down the small steps to get to the battered BMW.

Phoenix picked up the assault rifle and threw it in the back seats. As the vehicle was damaged on the outside, the interior still looked brand new.

Phoenix held up the pistol and emptied the clip. "What are you doing, Phoenix?" Darrell said as he saw her unloading the clip.

"We're not going to be fighting anybody else for a while. I'm going to finally put this all to rest."

"That's a good way to look at it," Darrell said.

Darrell started the vehicle, put it in reverse, drove towards the exit of the parking lot and turned left. Phoenix was expressing calmness and redemption. "To be honest with you, Phoenix, I've actually seen you one day when I was working," Darrell said.

"Where did you see me?"

"In the cafeteria, I also saw Warren, too. I noticed that you guys had a connection going on. You guys had something in common." Phoenix paused to think.

"What are you trying to say, Darrell?"

"I'm asking if you want to be friends?" Phoenix was surprised. Darrell let his arm out, "Friends?" Phoenix was hesitant. She was convinced and smiled, "Friends." They shook each other's hands.

"When we get back to work, you want to sit next to me at lunch? Just to talk, nothing else," Darrell said.

"I was about to ask the same thing. I could use someone to talk to once in a while." Darrell looked at Phoenix, "Your husband will be buried soon, that'll be your chance to say goodbye to him."

"I have to make it count, too," she said calmly, but felt sad on the inside. As Darrell was driving up the hilly roads, he saw the sun lighting up the skies in the horizon.

Chapter 14: A Day of Remembrance

July 26, 2019

There were white clouds that filled the sky, but weren't signs of a thunderstorm. Darrell entered Warren and Phoenix's road. He was still driving in the damaged BMW. He was wearing formal attire in all black except for his white dress shirt and was wearing a black tie. Darrell stopped and pulled into her driveway. He noticed her standing on the front porch. She expressed despair and had her hands by her stomach, carrying a bouquet of white flowers. She was wearing all black, which included a dress, a thin jacket and high heels.

As Darrell set the vehicle in park, Phoenix carefully walked down and approached his car. After she closed the door, she looked down. "You ready?" Darrell said, catching her attention. She didn't speak, she just looked at him. She was too emotionally torn to speak. Darrell set the vehicle in reverse and drove out of her driveway. He kept driving until he reached the highway. Phoenix slowly lifted her head up and looked out the window. She was looking at the sky and the vehicles passing on the opposite side of the road. Thoughts were going through her mind as she was thinking about flashbacks with Warren.

Darrell and Phoenix arrive at a graveyard. The interior shuts off as he takes the keys out. They open the doors and walk up the grassy hill towards the graveyard. They noticed a vast field of gravestones as some of them showed signs of aging, such as erosion and mild plant growth. They were looking around for Warren's gravestone as they peered their eyes around the graveyard. There wasn't really a funeral since he barely had a relationship with his family. Darrell spotted a fresh, white, clear gravestone in the center of the first row. "I

think that's Warren's over there," Darrell pointed to his left.

They slowly walk to his gravestone as Phoenix was still

carrying her bouquet.

As they approach Warren's gravestone, Darrell and

Phoenix read its contents. It read, "WARREN LEYTON, MARCH

17, 1993 - JULY 21, 2019". This made Phoenix bow her head

down in despair. She crouched and set the flowers down in

front of his gravestone. She looked at Warren's name. She

slowly placed her hand on the top of his grave and began

rubbing her hand around it. Phoenix cried as the pain was

building up inside of her, "I'm so sorry I couldn't protect you!"

She placed her hands over her face and kneeled to the

ground, pleading for Warren, "I want you back!"

Darrell walked towards Phoenix and crouched down

beside her. He looked at her and rubbed her back and gave

her a hug. Phoenix was crying on his shoulder. "Phoenix,"

Darrell said. She looked at him in the eyes. "He's in a better

place now." She felt so distraught as Darrell saw tears flow down her eyes. "Warren sacrificed his life for you, Phoenix. I know how it feels to lose a loved one. Think about the good times you had with him and what he's done for you and remember that he'll always be in your heart." Phoenix was still crying, but felt calm while listening to Darrell. She was hesitant, "You're right. I wouldn't know what I would've done without him. He was a great man."

"He loves you, Phoenix. When you go out at night, when the stars are out, look up and you'll see him up there in the heavens, watching out for you, to make sure you're safe." Darrell gave Phoenix another hug. "It's alright, Phoenix, you're not alone. It may feel like it, but it's not true." They stood up, but Phoenix couldn't leave just yet. She had one more thing to say to Warren, "I love you, Warren. I'll never forget you. Rest in peace."

Darrell and Phoenix are facing each other. "You going to be okay, Phoenix?" he asked.

"You know what? I think I'll be okay." She took a deep breath and smiled. "Come on," he said softly. They turned around and walked down the hill.

Darrell and Phoenix got back in the BMW and drove away from Warren's grave. He was going slow as the graveyard's speed limit was twenty miles per hour. He approached a stop sign and turned left to enter a road surrounded by trees on both sides. "Darrell," Phoenix said. "Thank you."

"You're welcome."

After Darrell drove away from the trees, they entered into a small part of town. Phoenix looked to her right and saw a white chapel, the same one that her and Warren married in, and smiled.

Chapter 15: One Year Later

July 26, 2020

On a warm, sunny morning at work, Darrell was driving

into the entrance of Parking Garage B. He was wearing a black

shirt with B&N Financing's company on it, blue denim jeans,

and his Starter brand tennis shoes. The BMW was fixed as it

looked like it just came out of the factory. Darrell did his daily

morning routine. Parking on the eighth floor, signing in at the

lobby, and ascending up to the seventeenth floor. He worked

in the financial branch of the company.

After working for three hours by his office desk, the bell

rings for Darrell's lunch hour. The offices haven't changed in appearance. He walked out of his office as the hallway immediately filled up with employees. He squeezed out of the hallway just in time, without causing concern to others, and walked to the elevator station. He walked to the elevator closest to him and descended to the lobby.

The elevator opened as Darrell saw people walking past the elevator as the lobby was scattered with employees. At least half of the employees were formally dressed while the other half were dressed like Darrell. The lunch line was quickly getting filled as he was approaching it.

As Darrell got in line, he looked to see Phoenix walking towards him. "Hey, Darrell," Phoenix said as she approached him.

"Hey, Phoenix, how are you?" Darrell smiled.

"Good, how are you?"

"Good." They were standing in line for the next ten minutes until they stood in front of the cafeteria doors. The lunch's menu was fruit and salad. The fruits were chopped strawberries and bananas while the salad was the classic iceberg, which contained lettuce, carrots, and radishes.

Darrell and Phoenix were standing in front of the kitchen counter with the same two chefs when Warren was still alive. The chefs were slightly aged, but still appeared young. They paid the usual two dollars and fifty cents for their lunches. "Thank you," Darrell and Phoenix said.

"You're welcome, have a good day!" The female chef said.

"You, too!" Phoenix said. They grabbed a milk bottle and walked down the small steps to sit at the table closest to them. They sit next to each other by the edge.

As Darrell was about to take his fork and eat his food, there was a loud bang that sounded, but it didn't come from the cafeteria. The bang startled and silenced everyone, including Phoenix and Darrell. He was staring at the cafeteria doors and kept a watchful eye.

Men in black wearing sunglasses walked in a fast pace into the cafeteria while concealing modified weapons. Everyone started panicking and screaming as they immediately jumped out of their seats. The three men fired assault rifles all around the cafeteria, already killing a couple people in the distance. The two chefs behind the kitchen counter ducked just before the men fired at them. The assault rifles had scopes attached to their sights. Two more men came in with pistols and shot a couple more people with armor piercing rounds, killing them instantly.

More men come into the cafeteria with various firearms, such as shotguns and machine guns and aimed them all at Darrell and Phoenix. The men formed a line. "Phoenix, come on!" Darrell yelled. The three men with the assault rifles continued to fire at the employees as the bullets scattered and ricocheted throughout the room. Most of the employees collapsed to the ground as the floor was smothered with blood.

As Darrell and Phoenix got up from the table, all of the men fired at them, missing them by mere inches. Darrell and Phoenix ran up to the guardrails of the lunch line and vaulted over them. They start running towards the back entrance door of the cafeteria. All of the men ran after them, initiating

in a lethal and critical pursuit.

TO BE CONTINUED

Writer's Note

The message that I'm trying to point out in this book is

by portraying the acts of friendship, strength, and sacrifice.

Life has a way of bringing surprises that most people don't

see coming. People also have many dreams as well. If you're

one of those people that have big dreams that are waiting to

happen, make it happen. Chase after it if you have to. If you

don't act upon your dreams, it'll eventually start to wither

away as every passing day goes by. That's why I chose to write

this book because I want to be something one day, someone

that people can look up to. I want to help people through

the hard times that we face as a whole today.

The violence in this world has been on the rise from the start. There are thousands among thousands of people that practice in gang violence, trafficking, and other problems like suicides from the problem of bullying. All it takes is one person to save many from a harmful situation, even if it's just an innocent bystander. I want to help people and inspire others to help those in need from the constant struggles we face today such was war, violence, and so forth. Everyone needs a hero sooner or later. The world is filled with a distorted perception that blinds the sight of many, but remember that there is always that sign of hope no matter what size it is and is always present whether visible or not. Writing this book was definitely a challenge to me.

After every page I've written, I've sacrificed most of my time and mainly focused on finishing this book. To all that just finished reading this book, I just want to say thank you for giving me your time. Always work towards what you desire and dream for because no matter what someone does, the world will always find ways to bring someone down until

they're close to nothing. So, accept the gift of life, because

you may never know what your life has in store for you.

Hello, my name is Travis Lee Heeter. I am a musician and an author.

Writing this book was a challenge to me as it was my first attempt on

actually writing one, but it definitely payed off in the end. For more

information on the book and myself, feel free to check out my social

media pages!

www.facebook.com/OfficialTravisHeeter

www.reverbnation.com/travisheeter

www.youtube.com/user/TravisHMusic

www.facebook.com/TheNumberConspiracy